ALSO BY MAGGIE ESTEP

Diary of an Emotional Idiot

SOFT MANIACS

Stories

MAGGIE ESTEP

Simon & Schuster

SIMON & SCHUSTER
Rockefeller Center
1230 Avenue of the Americas
New York, NY 10020

Designed by Sam Potts
Manufactured in the United States of America

1   3   5   7   9   10   8   6   4   2

Library of Congress Cataloging-in-Publication Data
Estep, Maggie.
Soft maniacs : stories / Maggie Estep.
p. cm.
1. United States—Social life and customs—20th century—Fiction.
2. Humorous stories, American. I. Title.
PS3555.S754S6 1999
813'.54—dc21   99-26941   CIP
ISBN 978-1-4767-9286-6

"Whoever's calm and sensible is insane."

Rumi

ACKNOWLEDGMENTS

Thanks to Anne Yohe, Andrew Vachss, Heather Schroder,
Geoffrey Kloske, Drew Hubner, and Marilyn Levy.
Thanks to Joe Andoe for painting Craig,
to Reginald for the fairy tales, and
to Donn Simmons for the neuroanatomy lessons.

Thanks in particular to everyone at Family Outing Productions—
Jenny Meyer, Stew Meyer, Shahram Victory, Chris Murray,
Jon Murray, Ellen Murray—without whose succor
I would surely unravel. Thanks also to Nancy Murray,
Neil Christner, Julia Murphy, Rick Moody, and Mark Ashwill
for the same.

CONTENTS

SOFT
MANIACS

HORSES

When my wife dumped me, I quit my job at the box factory, left Cleveland, and wandered for a few months. I didn't like my wife that much anyway. And I hated Cleveland.

At one point I was traveling with this guy Disco Donny. He had metal plates in his head. I'd met him at a flophouse I stayed in one night. We started hitchhiking together. He was pushing fifty. I don't know why he called himself Disco Donny.

Donny and I would find a day's work here and there, and at the end of the day I'd get drunk. Donny said he couldn't drink, though. It reacted badly with the plates in his head.

One day we were in this little town in Kentucky. We stopped in at a soup kitchen. A small, toothless guy eating next to us said we could get work hotwalking racehorses at a nearby farm. I'd had a thing for horses since I was a kid, so right away I was interested. Donny frowned, though. He stared at the toothless guy like this was some sort of trap.

"What's it to you?" Donny asked the little guy. "You get a cut or somethin'?"

The toothless guy stopped gumming his food for a moment and said "Huh?" like he had no idea what Disco Donny was talking about. And I'm sure he didn't.

When Donny and I left the soup kitchen, I told him I really wanted to go work with the horses. Donny frowned. He had unnaturally bright blue eyes that got black when he tried to think too hard.

"Yeah, okay, Leon," he said after a while. "If you want to." For some reason, Donny always called me Leon even though I kept telling him it was Leo, no *n*.

We walked to the farm the toothless guy had told us about. When we got there, Donny said I ought to hang back and he'd go find whoever was in charge. I guess I was pretty scraggly looking, and Disco Donny had this image of himself as really presentable even though he was anything but.

While Donny went to try and get us jobs, I stood there looking into the field where dozens of thoroughbreds were grazing, their coats shining like new dimes. One of them, a chestnut colt with white stockings, looked over at me. I made a soft noise in my throat. The colt pinned his ears forward but didn't come any closer. Just looking at him was soothing, though. I grew up in the sticks of Ohio, and whenever things got weird I'd go down the road to McCarthy's farm and ride their draft horses. Now, just the smell of horses can calm me down if I'm feeling strange.

After a few minutes, Donny came back shaking his head. "Nah, kid, we're too late. We gotta show up at four A.M. The guy said try back tomorrow."

I guess I looked as dejected as I felt because Donny socked me playfully on the shoulder and told me to cheer the fuck up, we'd come back the next day. Even when he meant to go easy,

Donny could really throw a punch, and so now my shoulder hurt on top of my other complaints, which, after four months' sleeping on benches, army cots, and boxes, were many. I looked over at the chestnut colt once more and then shrugged. I had a feeling we wouldn't make it back there the next day.

Donny and I walked out to the main road, heading back for town. I was dragging my feet and pretty soon Donny decided we ought to hitch a ride. We stopped walking and stuck our thumbs out.

A girl in a Buick convertible pulled over and right away I was suspicious. I'd never known a woman alone to pick up two scraggly males. But Donny just hopped right in. So I did too.

"Where you guys headed?" the girl asked us, and Donny told her we just wanted to go back to town.

This seemed to disappoint her, and at this point I noticed something was wrong with her face, like it didn't sit right on her bones. But she was wearing a short skirt and her legs were long and creamy so I stopped looking at her face and thought of how nice it would be if she suddenly veered off onto some dirt road and ordered me to go down on her. Donny could just sit there staring into space. He wouldn't mind.

Just as I thought this, Donny suddenly spoke up. "Look, a circus," he said loudly, pointing out a circus set up there by the side of the road. I looked over and sure enough, there were a bunch of striped tents, yellow and white but the yellow all faded. I could see a train of elephants marching along, making little clouds of dust rise up.

"Stop the car," Donny told the girl. She didn't seem to hear him, though. She just kept driving.

"Pull over NOW," Disco Donny shouted. The girl slammed on the brakes and her face started twitching as Disco Donny got out.

"Leon, come, we're going to the circus," he said to me. The

girl's twitching face was making me more nervous than Donny was, so I got out and followed him.

It was midmorning now and the circus people seemed to be just waking up. A fat lady emerged from a trailer. She was so huge that the trailer creaked with relief when she stepped out. She stood there for a second, looking around, then started jogging in place, her flesh slapping itself in protest. Nearby, some inbred-looking redneck guys were setting up a table of food as a burly man led an elephant by.

"I love the circus," Donny said. I shrugged. I wasn't that big on the circus. But it was nice to see Donny enthused like this.

We wandered around for about twenty minutes until a guy in a cowboy hat asked if he could help us with something.

"We're looking for work," Donny told the guy.

"That so?" the guy said, looking me and Donny up and down.

As it happened, the circus had a high turnover and the guy in the cowboy hat was hard-up for help. He hired us as ticket takers for the day, installing us on two stools by the main entrance and telling us we'd better not do anything stupid. When the guy had left, Donny started waxing rhapsodic about the circus. How it was all that was left that reminded him of the good ol' days. I wasn't sure what good ol' days, since from what I'd heard of Donny's past, there were only brief moments of good between long streaks of rotten luck. But Donny was happy. "This is great," he kept saying, rocking back and forth on his stool as people started coming in and handing us their tickets.

At one point Donny got beer from somewhere. I made a comment since he'd told me he couldn't drink—and I could have used a beer myself.

"Shut up, Leon," he said. So I did.

I don't know if it was the metal plates in his head or what, but a couple of beers did a number on Donny. He started rocking back and forth with increasing velocity, laughing this crazy, out-of-control laugh, showing teeth—and he didn't have good teeth. People were repelled over handing their tickets to us and eventually the guy who'd hired us came and fired Donny.

Donny got so angry he started throwing things. Change out of his pockets. Empty popcorn containers from the ground. The stools we'd been sitting on. There was an off-duty cop nearby and he got involved, whipping out handcuffs and telling Donny he'd better calm down. When Donny failed to settle, a few circus guys and the cop got behind him and snapped the handcuffs on. I tried to tell the cop Donny was a nice guy, he just had metal plates in his head. The cop just sneered at me, though, so I walked away. I figured Disco Donny probably wouldn't even notice I wasn't around anymore.

When they'd hauled Donny off, the guy who'd hired us came up to me. He was a pear-shaped guy with gaps between his teeth and a nose like a potato.

"What you doin' hangin' out with that character, son?" he asked me. I shrugged. He seemed to think I was a kid, even though I'd just turned twenty-five. Before I'd married Mickie and we'd moved to Cleveland, I'd lived in the sticks all my life, and I guess it made me look young.

The guy, whose name was Petey, brought me into the trailer he lived in with Gus, the elephant trainer. Gus was a lanky redheaded guy who looked dumber than a stamp until you saw his eyes. Then you noticed there was something in there. Gus fried up some hamburgers, and him and Petey shot the shit, grumbling about the murky weather and whatnot. I didn't say much but I was glad to be fed. A little later, Petey told me I could sleep in a spare stall in the animals' tent. At first, when he led me into the place, I confused the smell of elephants for horses and got excited because, since that afternoon, I'd gotten it into my head I needed to work with horses. But Petey told me there weren't any horses around.

I'd slept in all sorts of places, including a barn, but I'd never shared housing with elephants before. Hearing them foraging was sort of soothing, though. I bedded down on some straw and started thinking about the girl who'd picked me and Donny up. I pictured my hands on her creamy legs, digging into the flesh as I made my way up the short denim skirt she'd had on. I thought about flipping her over and kneading her ass cheeks and maybe entering her like that, from behind. Then I remembered the way her face had twitched, her lip curling up so it almost touched her nose. That put a damper on things. So I thought of my wife, Mickie, for a minute. She was always bossy sexually. Like I had to just lie there, like a rag doll, and let her do stuff to me. Which was okay for a while. Then she became bossy over everything else too. It got to where she'd go out all night and come back drunk, with her clothes fucked up, and wouldn't tell me where she'd been. But she would still want me to take off my clothes and lie there and let her do stuff. And I'd be there on my back with her mouth on parts of me and all I could do was wonder where she'd been all night. But I hadn't made a huge fuss about it. I figured she'd outgrow all that. Then, of course, she dumped me. Thinking about it depressed the hell out of me and I fell asleep.

In the morning, Petey set me to work helping Gus clean up after the elephants. Gus didn't say much and was fairly nice to work for. We fed the elephants, then led them into an outdoor pen while we mucked crap out of their stalls. Afterward Gus had a training session with the elephants and Petey got me doing odd jobs. Petey was both the manager and the handyman of the circus. Every few days, when the circus moved to a new town, something invariably went wrong and Petey had to take care of it. We fixed the toilet in the acrobats' trailer. We helped the roadies take knots out of a big rope that some disgruntled worker had tied up out of spite. We drove into town to get meat for the lions.

By afternoon everyone was getting ready for showtime. There were people walking around in clown suits and leotards, Gus was putting saddles on the elephants, the dog trainer was schooling his dogs. Pretty soon the crowds started coming, mostly poor families—kids in Kmart clothes, fleshy tired mothers, some of them with husbands in tow, blue-collar guys who wanted to be home watching the game. Nobody looked very happy. It seemed like coming to the circus was just something they were doing out of a sense of obligation, some vague historical recall of when circuses were the only entertainment there was. It was all sort of depressing, but in a nice way.

Once the show started up, Petey brought me in his trailer and offered me a beer. We sat there mostly silent, then he told me I could keep hanging around when the circus moved to the next town. I was pretty pleased.

Over the next few days I guess I made myself fairly useful. When we moved on into Lexington, one of the clowns got fired, so I was promoted. Being a clown had never been on my list of things to do, but a promotion is a promotion, so I went along with it.

The head clown, Remo, outfitted me with a costume: a nose, shoes, the whole bit. The first time I caught sight of myself in the mirror all kitted up like that, I just busted out laughing. I looked like some character out of a weird porno movie or a scary children's story. Like any minute I was gonna sprout an axe or a raging hard-on and go wreak clown havoc. Remo was standing right there and didn't understand why I was laughing so hard. To him there wasn't anything funny about being a clown.

Once I was outfitted, Remo and his wife, Fat Judy, showed me the basic routine: I had to ride in on an elephant, pretend to fall off, then do some somersaults. Remo and Fat Judy did most of the act. I was just there to thicken out the ranks.

The first night went fine. I rode in on Marty, the big Indian elephant. I fell off and did some somersaults. I went up into the audience and blew a horn and gave kids balloons. It beat working at the box factory.

Remo and Fat Judy gave me a tiny room of my own in their trailer, but I didn't get to spend much time there. When I wasn't working on new clown routines, I had to help out with the elephants. I didn't mind, though. The elephants reminded me of horses. They smelled different and didn't move a fraction as gracefully, but they were soothing all the same.

Things went along okay. Every two or three days we'd go to a new town. Sometimes there were circus groupies who'd linger after the show. They were the kind of girls who wanted to be rock band groupies, only no rock bands ever came through the dink towns we set up in, so these girls made do with the likes of us.

One night after the show, I hadn't even taken my clown outfit off when this Harley-looking chick came on to me. She was about four eleven, with tattoos and frizzy hair. She wasn't hideous. She came up and said, "Can I buy you a beer, dude?"

I didn't like being called "dude," so I said no and walked off.

I was passing by the lion tamer's trailer when I saw this girl I'd never seen before emerge. She was small, with dirty-blonde hair that hung in her face. The moment I laid eyes on her I started having visions of her thighs wrapped around my head. Of course, she didn't even notice me. She walked off toward where the roadies were taking down the main tent. And I just stood there, this guy in a clown costume, gawking at her and thinking lewd thoughts. But she was probably used to that.

The next day I pestered Remo and Fat Judy, asking them questions about the girl. They didn't know much but told me she was the lion tamer's daughter and she wasn't eighteen yet.

After that I started walking by the lion tamer's trailer about fifty times a day until finally, one night, Katie emerged. Her eyes were puffy and her hair was in nests like she'd been sleeping. All I could think was how I couldn't wait for her to be sleeping next to me.

I'd taken the clown costume off after the show and I was in jeans now. I walked over to where she was sitting in front of the trailer.

"Hi," I said.

"Who are you?" she said, squinting at me.

"The new clown."

"Oh."

"You wanna ride an elephant?"

She frowned but didn't say anything. She lit a cigarette.

"You're gonna hurt your little lungs," I said, staring at her chest.

"My lungs aren't that little," she said. "Where'd they find you, anyway?"

"What?"

"When'd you start working here?"

"Last week. In Kentucky," I told her. She was upsetting me. I felt like she could see inside my head, how I'd already mentally undressed her. My big lungs pressing against her little lungs.

"So you want me to ride an elephant, huh?" she mused, blowing a smoke ring. The way she said it, I instantly pictured her naked on the elephant.

And she might as well have been. She got on wearing only her cutoffs and a halter top. I figured that, being around the circus, she must have known about the fungus on the elephant skin, how you have to wear long pants or put a saddle on the elephant lest their skin fungus get on you and cause rashes. But I didn't say anything until after she'd dismounted. Then I mentioned she'd have to carefully wash the insides of her thighs. She made her eyes big. "Oh, really?" she said.

"Yeah," I said. "I'll help you, if you want." It was a pretty lame thing to say but she just shrugged. "Okay," she said.

I brought her over to Remo and Fat Judy's trailer, praying they weren't in there.

I opened the door and saw they were gone, and breathed easier. Remo and Fat Judy were very private and I didn't know how they'd take to me bringing Katie into their trailer.

"It's weird in here," Katie said, looking at the knickknacks Judy had in a little display case nailed to the wall. Both Judy and Remo had spent their whole lives on the road. And they'd made their trailer look like a cluttered suburban house. The place was festooned with lacy curtains, doilies, fake flowers, and embroidered pillows that Judy worked on during the hours of travel. She'd never learned how to drive and just sat there embroidering as Remo drove their trailer from town to town, week after week, year after year.

"They're nice people," I said, feeling protective of my hosts.

"Yeah, they're fine. But it's still weird in here," Katie said.

I led her into the tiny bathroom and started running water in the sink. I soaped up a washcloth and tried to seem totally in control of the situation. "Pull your shorts down," I told her.

"You do it," she said.

This made me nervous as hell. I don't know if she noticed, though. Her face had no expression. Like she was totally in the habit of telling guys to pull her shorts down. Which freaked me out. Maybe I wouldn't pull her shorts down right. Maybe dozens of guys before me had pulled her shorts down really efficiently.

She reached for my hand and put it on the button of her

shorts. She was totally in control of the situation. She was crucifying me.

My fingers fumbled with the button and she was just standing there, watching me. Eventually I got the button undone and tugged the shorts down. She had pointy little hipbones that jutted out, and a few stray pubic hairs were peeking out from her frayed white panties. I wanted to reach in and tidy them but I stopped myself.

I turned away from her and grabbed the washcloth. It was a flower motif washcloth. Fluffy and soft like everything else in the trailer. I got down on my knees and gently began rubbing the insides of Katie's thighs. She didn't move or make a sound. No matter how far up I let the washcloth go, Katie was impassive. I was melting and she was just watching. So I didn't make a single move. I washed the insides of her legs; then, using one of the pink hand towels, dried her off, pulled her shorts back up, and said, "There you go, girl."

She looked at me funny, then walked out of the trailer. Maybe she'd never talk to me again. But I figured now at least I had a chance. Maybe I'd kept her guessing and she wouldn't dump me as soon as we'd had sex. Of the nine women I'd slept with in my life, eight had dumped me after a few weeks. The only one who didn't was Mickie. And I married her. And then she dumped me.

I went into my tiny room. I put on a Townes Van Zandt tape Remo had loaned me and poured myself a shot of Jack. I lay down on my little mattress and listened to Townes's heartbroken voice tell stories. I stared at the ceiling. I felt like hitting my head against the wall. I heard Remo and Judy come in and I heard their Murphy bed creak in protest of Judy's weight as she sank down onto it. I drank another shot but it didn't do anything, so after a while I got up and went skulking by Katie and her dad's trailer.

The door was open and I could hear voices shouting. I got worried. I stood about twenty yards away, watching. After a minute, the father's girlfriend, a redhead I'd seen around, emerged. She was wearing a long slinky nightgown and she had a huge kitchen knife in her hand. She just stood there outside the trailer, holding the knife up like she was about to stab the air. I didn't know what to do. Then Katie's dad, Ben, popped his head out the trailer door. The girlfriend flipped around and jabbed Ben's face. Ben grabbed her wrists and got her to drop the knife, but she'd gouged him and he was bleeding. Ben stood perfectly still, just holding the girl's wrists and staring at her, as if willing her back to her senses. After a minute she just put her arms around his neck and rested her head on his shoulder. Then he picked her up and carried her back in the trailer. Right away I wanted to go pull Katie out of there, but I didn't know how wise that was. So I just stood there, rooted to my spot.

After a while the lights went off in the trailer and I walked over and picked up the knife the girlfriend had dropped. I wiped it off, then went back to sit in my spot. I planted the knife next to me in the earth and just kept staring at that trailer. When dawn finally came, I went and knocked on the door. I was going to demand to see Katie. I knocked and knocked, and finally Katie herself opened up.

"What?" she said, rubbing her eyes. She was wearing a long T-shirt and nothing else.

"Here's your dad's knife back," I said, offering the knife.

"Oh," she said, not even asking where I'd gotten it. Like this happened all the time.

"You wanna ride the elephant again?" I said then.

"What time is it?"

"Pushing six," I told her, glancing over at the sun coming up behind a hill.

"What are you, a guy that can tell time from looking at the sky?"

"Yeah, wanna make something of it?"

She laughed. She had lovely small teeth and a wide mouth.

"I don't think the elephants are awake yet, Leo," she said.

"They won't mind."

She said, "Okay," then disappeared back in the trailer. When she came out, she'd put her cutoffs and tank top on and grabbed a cup of coffee. She offered me a sip, which I took.

She lit a cigarette as we walked over to get Marty the elephant out from his stall. I made her wait outside since she was smoking.

Once we'd led Marty to the pen and I'd gotten Katie up on his back, I started asking her about the crazy redhead.

"Oh, that's my dad's girlfriend, Jody. She's a rich girl. Met my dad and dropped out of college. She's sort of neurotic," Katie said.

"You get along with her?" I asked.

"I get along with anybody."

"Oh yeah?"

"Sure," she said. She was swinging her legs back and forth at the elephant's sides now, but Marty seemed to like it. He had a particularly peaceful expression on his face. Like even a big old elephant could appreciate having this cute girl on top of him.

"I have a kid sister Alfie, but she stayed with my mom when my parents split up. So when Jody's not acting all crazy, it's almost like having a sister again. She does get nutty sometimes, though. I just keep away from her then. When she's nice she can be sweet as hell. I guess most crazy people are like that."

"Is she nuts nuts, like she's been in loony bins?"

"Nah, she's rich people nuts. You know, just neurotic. But she really is sweet."

"Oh." I shrugged.

I watched her ride the elephant.

When she'd had enough, she got down and walked toward me.

"I guess I forgot to put long pants on," she said, her face totally solemn.

"I guess you did," I said.

We walked the elephant back to his stall and then I brought Katie with me into Remo and Fat Judy's trailer. They were still sleeping so we tiptoed into the bathroom. I ran the water, knelt in front of Katie, and tugged her shorts down. When I looked up, she was pulling her halter top off.

"Do my whole body," she said.

"What?"

"Wash my whole body," she said, then peeled her underpants off too.

I hesitated.

"What's the matter, you scared of me?" she jibed.

I grabbed her shoulders and turned her so her back was to me as I soaped up the washcloth, and starting at the nape of her neck and going down, went over every inch of her. At one point I had her bent forward over the sink with her little ass poking out at me as I washed between her legs. I felt a shiver pass through her.

I dried her off and dressed her. She looked at me for a moment, then walked out.

I went into my room and just stood there, not knowing what to do. I didn't have to work for another few hours. I was exhausted but revved up. I pulled my fifth of Jack out from my bag and had a few shots. I thought about Katie on the elephant. I thought about Katie in the bathroom. I jerked off. I drank some more. I guess eventually I passed out. When I came to, Katie was in my bed.

"What are you doin'?" I asked her. I saw she had a T-shirt on but her shorts were in a pile on the floor. She started kissing my stomach, then letting her lips trail down, making a dewy path to my hard-on.

For some reason it pissed me off. Like she would have done all this without waking me up if she could have. I was totally incidental in the whole equation.

"Get offa me," I told her.

This just made her laugh, though.

"Katie, stop it. We've got to talk."

"What do you want to talk about?" she said, straddling me. This shut me up. I grabbed her hips and flipped her underneath me and dove inside her in this fierce way that scared the shit out of me.

After that, we got along okay.

When fall came the circus went farther south, through Louisiana over to Texas, then back east, into Georgia and down through Florida. The towns we traveled through started blurring together. I worked. I washed Katie's thighs. I fucked Katie. I loved Katie. I don't know if she loved me. There was a part of her I never seemed to reach. She was like this little savage; hadn't gone to school since ninth grade and had mostly raised herself since she'd left her ma and come to live with her father at the circus. I guess living like this had made her the way she was. Never having roots and whatnot. She didn't operate under the normal conventions of things. I seemed to be her boyfriend, but I wasn't sure. She never said the things women were supposed to say to men. As for her father, he didn't talk to me, but neither did he seem to mind about me and Katie. Besides, we never saw much of him anyway. Katie and I always slept in my little alcove in Remo and Fat Judy's trailer. They liked Katie and I guess they liked me.

One night, near Jacksonville, Florida, Katie and I were lying out behind the elephant pen. We'd had sex a bunch already and now we were both tired. Katie was lying on her back, smoking a cigarette.

"I wish they'd bring the horses back," she said.

"What horses?"

"There used to be a horse guy. A trick rider. But he was a junkie and he got fired. He'd let me ride his horses, though."

"Did you fuck him too?" I asked, surprising myself. Up to that point I'd liked how we didn't talk about our past or make big promises for the future.

She looked at me for a minute and then smiled. "Sure," she said, flicking her cigarette toward the moon.

"You did?" I sat up and stared at her.

"Sure."

"How many people have you had sex with?"

"Twenty-eight."

"WHAT?"

"I'm kidding. I didn't fuck the horse guy. Don't be a jerk."

"You fucked that trapeze guy last year."

"How'd you know that?"

"Gus told me."

"Gus is just mad cause it wasn't him," she said, lighting another cigarette.

"You smoke too much. And you did."

"Did what?"

"Fuck the trapeze guy."

"So?"

"So, nothing," I said.

"What are you trying to prove?" she asked, propping up on her elbow.

"Nothing. Just don't do it with anybody else."

"Like I was going to?"

"How do I know?"

"You should just know," she said, putting her hand right over my heart.

That shut me up for a minute.

She was right. I should have known, but I was scared. She kept talking about how when she turned eighteen she was moving to New York City to take pictures. Lately she'd started using crazy Jody's camera and taking pictures of people's arms and legs. They were weird pictures but they were kind of beautiful, and I guess Katie had decided she had to move to the city and be around other people who took pictures. I started having the feeling I'd had with women in my past. Like I was losing her. So I'd started doing all this stuff to try and keep her interested. A few weeks earlier, in the middle of the night, I'd tied her hands behind her back, blindfolded her, put her in Gus's truck, and driven her to a nearby beach. I took her out of the truck, led her to the ocean, and pushed her ahead of me into the surf. When we were in up to our shoulders I started fucking her, with the ties and blindfold still on and the ocean crying in our ears. That got her attention.

Now, lying there, staring at her bare stomach, I got an idea.

"We're going to ride a horse," I told her.

"What are you talking about?" she said.

"When we pulled into town yesterday I saw a horse farm down the road. We're gonna go ride some horses now," I told her.

"We're just gonna go ride some strangers' horses?"

"Uh-huh."

"Okay," she said, standing up and pulling her shorts out of her crotch.

It took us close to forty minutes to walk there, but it was a nice night with a wet velvet sky hanging low over our heads.

We finally came to the horse farm, and right away I noticed a gray Percheron out in the field. He was a nice solid workhorse, the kind that wasn't likely to make much fuss over a stranger taking him for a midnight ride.

He put his ears forward when I walked up to him. I put my hand out, palm first, for him to sniff, and he licked it. I put my nose up to his neck and breathed in the smell of him. I felt my whole body relax.

I told Katie to go into the barn and find a bridle. She came back a few minutes later with a halter and lead rope in hand.

"It was dark as shit in there and the sheep started bleating, so I just grabbed this," she said, handing me the halter. She'd run to the barn and back and was panting a little now, her mouth slightly open, like a tired puppy. I kissed her, then I put the halter on the horse, led him over to the fence, and climbed on his back. I squeezed his sides and asked him to walk forward. It felt so good to be on a horse. All these knots in me started unraveling. And I felt like I could hold on to Katie like this, if she could see me, really see me like this.

Once I was sure the horse would take pretty much anything in stride, I steered him back over to the fence and told Katie to get on behind me. She wrapped her arms around my waist. I felt like we'd been sucked into another world. A place where I had power over things and situations.

The moon was hanging like a dinner plate as I asked the horse for a trot. We bounced along for a minute. Katie held on to me.

"Get him to gallop," she said in my ear.

Riding a strange horse bareback in the middle of the night was fool enough, never mind galloping. I knew that. But it didn't seem to matter. It didn't seem like anything could go wrong. So I asked the horse to canter and, a few strides in, to stretch into a gallop.

I didn't see the fence coming but the horse did. I suddenly

felt him hit a spot and soar. He must have cleared the fence by two feet. I spun in slow motion through the air. I saw the night twinkling as I somersaulted and collided chin first with the ground.

Next thing I knew, Katie's face was in front of mine and she was saying my name over and over. I opened my eyes and the worry I could see creasing her brow made all the pain go away. For a minute, anyway. Then my chin was on fire and my foot throbbed like crazy. All the same, I made Katie go round up the horse and get him safely back in his field.

Once I could stand up I leaned on Katie and we hobbled out to the road. Katie was being sweet, but I had a sense I'd fucked something up. I'd tried to show her how I had power in the world but all I'd done was bust up my foot and endanger her own life.

After a long time, a car finally passed on the road. A tired old farmer gave us a ride to the nearest hospital.

My foot was badly broken and I couldn't work as a clown or do anything more than be a ticket taker. After a week, Remo and Fat Judy had to hire a new clown—who moved into their trailer, displacing me. Remo felt bad about it but there was nothing he could do. I wouldn't be able to walk for at least two months.

Katie got her father to let me move in with them. When she told me this news, I just said, "Oh, cool." I was excited, though. I had the idea that sharing a domestic life would make her want to stay with me.

The first night, I cooked dinner for her and her dad and crazy Jody. I made meatloaf and mashed potatoes. Katie made chocolate pudding for dessert. By the time we all crowded around the tiny kitchen table, though, Ben and Jody had been drinking a lot and were fighting. Katie and I shoveled food down our throats as those two bickered. Jody was accusing Ben of flirting with one of the acrobats. Ben just kept shaking his head, saying, "You're crazy, girl."

Finally, after Ben had told Jody she was crazy for about the fifth time, she dumped her plate over his head and stormed out of the trailer. Ben just sat there with food dripping down his face and poured himself another drink.

Katie and I cleaned up the kitchen and neither of us said anything to Ben. I guess we both felt bad for him, but it's not like we'd made him pick such a lunatic for a girlfriend. We went back into Katie's room, and as soon as we'd shut her door she ripped my pants off and started blowing me, and somehow it seemed so damned twisted, her dad sitting there on the other side of the thin door, his girlfriend wandering around somewhere, and Katie going down on me with this fury, like all the emotional havoc she felt living in this environment was now getting taken out on my dick. Which wasn't so bad.

My foot was healing but not fast enough, and I was starting to go crazy being cooped up most of the time. Katie was out at all hours now, taking pictures of people's arms and legs. Every town we pulled into, she went looking for new arms and legs. In a way, it was worse than her having sex with other people.

Then one night Jody totally went off the deep end. Anytime she got it into her head that a woman had looked at Ben she'd get drunk and start playing with the kitchen utensils. Mostly the knives, but I'd also seen her threatening Ben with a fork. This particular night, Ben had gotten clawed by one of the lions and had to go to the hospital. When Jody and Katie went to pick him up, a nurse was sitting on the side of Ben's bed. Which sent Jody over the edge.

As soon as they got back to the trailer, Jody started having a fit, screaming at Ben, chasing him around, then pouring about half a fifth of Jack down her throat in one gulp. Nothing anyone said made a dent in her tantrum. At one point she was lying on the kitchen floor twitching and wailing like an epileptic infant. Eventually Ben called an ambulance. They sedated Jody and carted her off.

The trailer was wrecked. Ben was wrecked. Katie and I went into her room and just lay there, stiff as boards next to each other. Seeing something like that didn't exactly make you feel sexy.

The next day the circus moved on into the Palm Beach area, and two days into our stint there, Jody returned to us, escorted by her parents, a pair of very tall and hostile-looking people who, it turned out, were both psychiatrists. The father had no hair and a long face like Lurch from *The Addams Family.* The mother was long too. Not her face so much as her body. Really narrow and tense looking. They stood on each side of Jody, like parentheses. They'd walk with her from one end of the trailer to the other as Jody picked stuff up and threw it in a duffel bag. No one said anything. At first I'd actually tried engaging the father in conversation. I asked had he ever been to Florida before. He looked at me coldly and said, "Of course," then turned his back to me.

When Jody had gotten all her stuff, the mother said, "Is that everything, Jody?" and Jody shrugged.

Ben was nowhere to be found, so only Katie and I were there to say good-bye. Katie and Jody hugged each other, and I saw how tense Jody's body was when Katie put her arms around her. Like the parents' stiffness had suddenly infected Jody too.

And then they were off. Katie and I watched Jody get in the backseat of the white rental car. Neither of us said anything. I couldn't tell if Katie was sad or relieved. Probably both.

After about an hour Ben reappeared. He was pale as hell and acted weird the rest of the day. That night, at showtime, both Katie and I stood backstage watching him do his act. We were worried that Ben was so upset the lions would smell it on him and maim him. Katie's fingers dug into my arm as Ben put his head inside Koko, the biggest lion's, mouth. Ben got through the show okay, though, and afterward Katie was incredibly attentive to him.

In fact, all the next week Katie was so attentive to Ben she barely talked to me. Mostly I sat listening to Remo's Townes Van Zandt tape over and over: *My days they are the highway kind / they only come to leave.* Which about summed it up. I got pretty down and I started to really need to see some horses.

One night I had a few drinks. Maybe a few too many. I still couldn't walk on my foot and I didn't feel like dealing with anyone to borrow their car, so I got Marty the elephant out and rode him down the road, looking for a farm that had horses. I don't remember exactly what happened, but evidently I was riding Marty right in the *middle* of the road. A truck came barreling along and, swerving to avoid Marty, ran off the road. The driver wasn't killed but the truck exploded.

I ended up in jail overnight. When Katie and Ben, looking none too thrilled, came to bail me out, I knew I'd just driven the last nail in the coffin of what Katie and I had had. When we got back to her room I sat down on her little bed and started rubbing my foot that I'd ended up walking on during the whole ordeal. Katie had her back to me and was standing in front of the mirror, solemnly brushing her hair. I'd never seen her brush it before. Usually it just hung down her back in nests.

"Your hair looks good brushed," I said to her back. She just shrugged and kept brushing.

The circus was about to pack up and move on into North Carolina. I had to stay here in Charleston to appear in court. I told Katie I'd catch up with them in a few days.

"I think you might be in trouble, Leo," Katie said.

"Yeah?"

"I don't know if you're gonna be coming back to the circus."

"And that doesn't bother you?"

"It bothers me," she said, looking me in the eyes for the first time in weeks. "A lot of things bother me but that doesn't mean I can do much about it. I'm going to New York in two weeks anyway. So I won't be around."

"You're going to New York City? In two weeks?" I felt stabbed.

"I gotta get on with my life. I'm not a circus person."

"And I am?"

"I don't know what you are, Leo. I think you drink too much, though."

"Everybody drinks too much."

"I don't."

"I'm coming with you," I said.

"To New York?"

"Yes."

"No you're not."

"Says who?"

"You're just not, Leo. You're not a city person."

"I thought you said you didn't know what I was."

"Well, I don't. But you're not a city person."

She was right. The only city I'd ever lived in was Cleveland and it had been too much. The thought of New York actually made me sick to my stomach. But how could she be so composed about it. It was like the first time I'd washed her off after the elephant ride. The way she'd just stood, utterly still, as I rubbed the soft skin of her inner thighs.

I sat there looking at her back. She just kept brushing her hair. I got up and hobbled into the bathroom. I ran some water and soaped up a washcloth. I went back into Katie's room. I came up behind her. I put one hand on her hip while I unfastened her jeans with the other. I looked at us reflected in the mirror, my hands pulling the jeans over her hips. She met my eyes in the mirror and for the first time I saw the impossible sadness that was buried under her veneer, and I wanted to fuck it out of her. I bent her forward and she planted her arms against the wall and stuck her beautiful ass in the air as I peeled off my pants and entered her. At one point she turned over to look at me and I saw things in her face I'd never seen before. A sort of kaleidoscope of emotions. And it wrecked me, to see her like this, to know I was losing her for good, to know more than anything that the reason I could see into her this way was that it was the last time we'd do this.

A few hours later, I stood there like a dolt, watching the caravan of all the circus trailers and vans pulling out of the camp. Katie was in her dad's trailer. Probably lying on her bed. I don't know. She didn't get up and peer out the window to get one last look at me.

I went to court and was remanded to rehab.

I arrived in a bus with a dozen other drunks. A nurse strip-searched me, then sent me up to a little room with plastic sheets on the bed. I guess they thought I'd shit myself when the DTs hit. I didn't, but I saw some pretty odd stuff. I didn't sleep for a few days and my blood pressure skyrocketed. I never thought I drank enough to merit anything like this, so I was pretty surprised.

On the fifth day they put me in a dormitory cabin with four-teen other guys and I had to start participating in the whole rigmarole. Up at six, make the bed, shower, breakfast, group therapy, one-on-one therapy, lunch, A.A. meeting, arts and crafts, and so on. They didn't leave you alone for five minutes.

The other guys were mostly older than me. Worn old men who smelled like bad dreams. I didn't really talk to anybody except in group therapy, where you got demerits if you didn't speak up.

One day I was sitting on the steps by the main building, just looking at the grass and trying not to think. A station wagon pulled in with three new rehab inmates. I saw that one of the guys was in a straitjacket and was apparently refusing to go inside. He started kicking at the counselors who were trying to bring him in to the nurse's station. When the guy turned around, I realized it was Disco Donny.

Donny didn't remember me but liked me all the same. I asked him where he'd been and he frowned at me, like I was out of line for asking. But maybe he just didn't remember.

When we got out of rehab, Donny and I started hitchhiking together again. I told him I thought we should go get jobs working with horses. He didn't care either way, so we made it down to Kentucky, and just outside of Versailles we found a farm that hired us as hotwalkers.

The barn was painted a bright blue-green that matched the grass of the rolling hills around it. That first morning of work I got stepped on, bitten, and kicked by a series of high-strung colts I had to cool down after their workouts. And it made me feel better than anything had in ages.

Donny and I met up at lunch break and compared notes.

"I like these horses," Donny said, his blue eyes turning black like he was thinking hard, trying to articulate something that just wasn't coming.

"Horses are soothing," I said. Then for some reason I started telling Donny about Katie. I didn't know if he was listening to me. He just kept staring out into the field where the yearlings were grazing. I told Donny how much I'd loved Katie. After a minute Donny looked up and shrugged.

"I had a girl," he said, "before they brought me up to that rehab place. Lisa. Beautiful girl. Worked as a whatdyacallit. Beauty person. We got along good and she let me move into her place. It was nice having a home and a woman and I tried to treat her good. But one day, I don't know. Something got into me and I went out and got a beer. After that I got another beer. Then a few more. I came back to Lisa's place and Lisa wasn't home yet and I needed some money. I looked around and there wasn't any money anywhere, so I started trying to think of what I could sell to get some money. The only thing Lisa had worth anything was these fish. These big tropical fish. Lisa was crazy for fish. So I get a plastic bag and I scoop two of the fish out and I go on over to the pet store to sell the fish. Those fish cost almost a hundred bucks a pop and I'm telling the guy he can give me twenty bucks for the fish, but he's not going for it. I try the other pet store but they don't even sell fish at that store. So finally I give up. I go home. Lisa's home and she's freaking out 'cause the first thing she does when she comes home from work is look at the fish. So then she sees me with the fish in the plastic bag. She grabs the bag out of my hand and then she starts screaming, 'cause I guess it killed the fish to be in that bag all afternoon. I feel awful. I feel worse than I ever felt, 'cause I liked Lisa. But after she was done screaming she just didn't say anything at all. She didn't tell me I had to move out, she just stopped talking to me. Two weeks I stuck around but Lisa wouldn't talk to me no more. She just took care of the one fish she had left. That and went to work at the beauty place. One night I got so upset about it I went drinking, and it was bad with the metal plates in my head. So I guess I went crazy and then I ended up at the rehab place,"

Donny said, shaking his head, then staring off at the horses in the field.

I made some sort of sympathetic noise.

"Nah," Donny said then, looking at me, "it's okay. I get along with horses better than women anyway."

"Yeah," I said, "I guess I do too."

THE PATIENT

I had a rambling apartment in Brooklyn and I fucked my girl-friend Jody in every part of it. So did a lot of other people. One time, I came home, she was going at it with this saggy old dyke that had a cane. The dyke was on her knees and her flesh hung off her in folds. She had her mouth buried in Jody's bush. Communing there. The dyke had one hand on Jody's ass and the other resting on the cane that she held out to the side.

When I came closer, Jody looked at me and smiled, her tiny perfect teeth gleaming like miniature Chiclets. Jody winked at me, pulled the old crone's face out of her crotch, looked at her, and said: "Millicent, I'd like you to meet my boyfriend, Rob."

Millicent's fleshy mouth grinned up at me, and the gnarled hand, the one resting on the cane's carved head, did this weird squeezing motion.

It was the most revolting thing I've ever seen in my life. I got a hard-on right away.

"You don't mind, baby, do you?" Jody said, tilting her head and opening her eyes at me wide.

I just shrugged and grunted. I went to stand behind Jody. I rubbed against her bare ass and sniffed at the back of her neck.

By now, Jody had brought the Crone's face back into her crotch, and with her free hand she reached behind and unzipped me. "That's my boy," Jody said, taking my cock and wedging it into her ass.

Jody was exceptional in many ways. Not least of these her ability to climax from anal sex. Even without clitoral stimulation. Of course, in this instance she had a lot of that going on. That Crone's tongue was like some weird reptile's, darting, blue, and hard. It must have worked wonders, though. Or I did. Jody came so violently she fell forward onto the floor, causing me to lose my balance and land right on top of the Crone.

And so, I fucked the Crone too. It was one of the most horrific things I ever experienced. I don't think she'd had anything in there, including a tampon, in a good decade. The woman had to be pushing sixty. She was dry as a bone as I wedged my way in.

Jody managed to get over her waves of coming and was sitting up now. She rubbed her hand between her legs, then reached down and applied this moisture onto the Crone's crotch. This repulsed me further but facilitated things a great deal. And for some reason caused the Crone to start laughing. The whole flesh sack of her started trembling with this laughter. Which made me shoot into her. Hard.

• • •

I don't know what happened then. I probably went and scrubbed my cock with a Brillo pad. And Jody did god knows what. She had this way with all these horrible people she fucked. A bedside manner, if you will. I'd witnessed it before as I hung around the kitchen, listening to the shrieks and whip sounds coming from the bedroom as my girlfriend debased strangers, their lusty cries rising up like a devil's sonata. And afterward, when these willing victims emerged from the bedroom, shaken and spent, I'd seen Jody blind them with a smile and a kind word, making them glad for getting used like disposable sets of genitals. Glad for never even getting acknowledged by Jody if and and when she ran into them somewhere. Jody had charisma.

She was leggy, with no tits and red hair that hugged her little head. She had an acrobat's body and a nymphomaniac's insatiability. But she wasn't quite a nympho. She was a doctor. Or at least on her way to being one.

Some weeks Jody shot speed and studied those psych tomes for days on end. She had such focus. Pausing only to jerk off and suck her thumb. I wasn't allowed to fuck her during these jags. Afterward, though, when she'd passed some test with flying colors, she'd go on a sex binge. She'd take me along to sex clubs, where she'd sit in these dank chambers, sucking her thumb, playing with herself, and looking twelve as she watched people beating, sodomizing, and eating one another. Everyone went nuts for Jody. Men, women, *anything* tried to fuck her as she sat there jerking off and watching the goings-on. She made me suck dicks and fuck monstrous women. She had a dog lick me once. She tied me up. She rammed zucchinis up my ass. She beat me.

She was incredible, and I loved her.

The thing that ruined everything had to do with the dyke Crone with the cane.

Somehow, and I don't know how, Jody ran into that old Crone again. God only knows where she'd found her in the first place. Some mental clinic at Bellevue on rounds or something. I don't know. But Jody actually ran into her and it transpired the Crone was knocked up. That's right. That old bag had a baby in her and I'd had something to do with it. Well, I'd had everything to do with it. Turns out I was the only guy that'd been up that disused love canal since 1963.

Now you'll get what I'm doing here. When I tell you the rest of it.

So Jody comes back one day and tells me this story about the knocked-up crone. Now Jody, for all her charms, was psychotic, so I just thought she'd shot too much speed or something. There was no way that Crone could be pregnant. Just impossible. And I put it out of my mind. Until one day I come home from work and the Crone is in there. In *my* apartment. Lying on *my* bed, wearing only white cotton briefs. It was vile. She had her large feet propped up on some pillows and Jody was all done up in this sexy outfit, solicitously leaning over the Crone. And, you guessed it, that Crone was very obviously knocked up. It was so fucking hideous. Worse even than fucking her. Her nipples were the size of dinner plates, and blue veins stood out and throbbed like gorged flower stems.

I mean, fuck that, right? I'm a nice Jewish boy from Chicago. I made good grades in high school. I loved my high school girlfriend but we broke up right before college. I dated a few different women at Princeton but none of them moved me very much. Then, once I had a BFA, I got a job in Manhattan working as assistant to Frederico Malodorio, the Italian painter. I started to meet some amazing women. And then Jody. She was hanging around Frederico's studio one day. She was lying on his couch and she was wearing this very proper sort of Upper East Side outfit. Navy and yellow. Tan pantyhose. I came in, back from running to Balducci's to get Frederico that fucking special goat cheese he had to have on his salad. I handed the grocery bag to Frederico.

"Rob, meet Jody," Frederico said, waving a hand in the direction of the couch. Jody was lying on her side. She had her knee-length skirt hiked up to midthigh, and from where I was standing I could see she didn't have any underwear on under her pantyhose. But this isn't even what got me interested. No. She was gorgeous but there was this lost look in her eyes, like this stray-kitten look, as she smiled at me sweetly and told me how nice it was to meet me.

A few minutes later, when Frederico told me I could leave for the day, I figured it was 'cause he needed to get busy with Jody. So I was really surprised when she followed me out onto the street.

"Would you like to go for a walk?" she blurted out, all shy and nervous seeming, not at all like the kind of girl who lounges on some sex maniac painter's couch revealing her crotch to the world.

And I told her, "Sure, I'd love to," and don't you know, that's exactly what we did: walked. All the way to the East River park. We sat on a bench. And the whole time she was still acting shy, sweet, vulnerable. She sat next to me demurely, knees drawn together. We watched boats on the water and thugs walking their pitbulls. She told me some of her story.

She was the daughter of two prominent psychiatrists. Had been pressured into becoming a doctor herself and rebelled against it. Dropped out of Vassar and dropped acid and went to live with some touring circus for a while. Then eventually got the calling. To be a shrink. She thought it'd help her understand things better, she told me. Understand herself. The world. She finished up premed at Columbia and now was at the end of med school.

We didn't even touch each other that first day. Afterward, when I went back home, I realized I was stuck on her.

So when, after a few more dates, she ripped into me sexually, although I thought she was a little maniacal, a little devoid of any restraint at all, I didn't let it worry me. Quite the contrary. I counted my blessings to have found a girl who had a vulnerable side yet could fuck like the Marquis de Sade.

She moved in after a month. She started bringing strangers home after two months. Sure, I was shocked, horrified at first. But it didn't have anything to do with our relationship, really.

Now we'd been together a year, and it was stormy but good. Good until this whole Crone thing happened.

Jody didn't even ask. She just moved the Crone into my apartment. The Crone's girlfriend had kicked her out or something. If you believe a thing like that could even have a girlfriend. And I had to go along with it. I figured eventually Jody would get sick of the whole situation and kick the Crone out, and Jody and I would get back to normal. So I just let it be.

In the day, I'd go off and work for Frederico. Everything's cool, I'm meeting all these people, I get two drawings in a group show, women are coming on to me, men are coming on to me, the world is pouring itself over me like honey. I'm not interested in anyone but Jody, though. And each night I go home to her. I go home to my girl and her Crone. And things are getting increasingly weird. I'm not sure Jody's even showing up at med school. She's stopped shooting speed and even smoking cigarettes, like it's her body that's carrying the baby. She's gone all macrobiotic, and she and the Crone sit around reading natural childbirth guides and going to Lamaze classes. Forget about Jody coming out to dinner or a club or something, never mind letting me fuck her.

But that was the problem with Jody. I couldn't say no to her. Even when she's got this knocked-up ninety-year-old lesbian living in my apartment, carrying this *thing* that is, to my horror, a part of me, this *thing* that will doubtless pop out malformed and shrieking, this *thing* that will have the Crone's sagging flesh and my eyes, this *thing* the thought of which makes my skin crawl as nothing ever has, even when Jody's devoting her every breath to this unborn *thing* and the belly that holds it, even when Jody is barely talking to me, I love her. I love her with every fiber of my being.

Things kind of degenerate then. The Crone's about to have the kid and Jody is all worried that we don't have enough money to get all the baby things the Crone and the *thing* will need. Every time I come home from work, Jody has sold off something else. First it's my mother's engagement ring. I don't even know how Jody found it. My mother had sent it to me because I was getting ready to pop the question to Jody. That is, before the Crone moved in. After the ring it's the stereo and VCR, and pretty soon Jody's sold off all the normal furniture and amassed all this baby stuff. Like the whole apartment has become a nursery. I start to think maybe this is too much. No one ever made me feel the way Jody did, but enough's enough.

One day I come home ready to rip Jody out of there and force her to go outside with me and talk. But the Crone's nowhere in sight and Jody is lying on the bed, outfitted in thigh-high stiletto boots and a white bustier with a string of pearls around her neck. And she opens her arms wide and says, "Baby, I've missed you."

I just melt. I mean, just like that. Like all this weird stuff hasn't happened. Like she's just my girl, my beautiful crazy Jody. I love the way her tits fail to fill out her bustier. I love the way the thong in the back separates her moon-crescent butt cheeks. I love how wet she is when I stick my fingers inside her. Her whole body arches as I bite her nipple through the bustier. She starts ripping my pants off then, frantic, possessed.

I ram myself into her and it's the best feeling I've ever had in my life.

"Baby, I need you," I whisper at her, looking in her eyes and gently sliding in and out of her.

"I know," she says.

Things start to build. We haven't done this in so long. I've watched her fawn over that Crone for months now and it's all welling up in me, like this enormous balloon.

I pull out of her. She peels off one of her boots and flips me over onto my stomach.

"Take this, my love," she says, sticking the heel of the boot in my ass. I come just as the thing rips me. But it's not enough. I need more of her. More and more. I eat her. I devour her. She comes like fifteen times.

Even when the Crone gets home later that night, slagging her huge belly in front of her, I almost don't mind. I almost feel warmly toward that Crone and the *thing* that's now kicking up a storm inside her huge old stomach, and I even go so far as to *touch* the Crone's stomach when she asks me do I want to feel *my* child moving inside of her and the Crone has pulled up her maternity dress, and I put my hand on that weathered belly now distended with life and I feel the *thing* kick, and instead of feeling warm fuzzy paternal feelings, I feel nauseous and I quickly turn away lest my lunch revisit me, and I can feel both the Crone and Jody boring holes in my back with their eyes, eyes that are milked over with a weird love for the *thing,* and it's all pretty sick and awful and I know I should just leave, but I can't, I refuse.

And then, two days later, Jody leaves me.

I come home from work. All the nursery furniture's gone.

Everything's gone and there's this fucking note. The Crone's gone into labor and they're going to the hospital and then they're going to live on their own. With the baby. I shouldn't try to find them. They'll find me. When the time's right.

And that's what did me in. She fucking left me. I loved her. I put up with everything she could dish out, which you'll have to admit was a lot. And she left me.

So I guess I lost it a little. I guess I turned up on the maternity ward at the hospital looking for them, trying to figure out which one was the *thing*. You know how they have that glass partition and all the happy parents stand there gazing through at their little shrively offspring. So I get in there and I'm looking through the glass, trying to pick out which one is the *thing*, right, trying to stake it out, half expecting to see it with red glowing eyes, like Rosemary's fucking baby or something.

I've got this Colt .45 in my gym bag. Some freak who buys a lot of Frederico's paintings, he's like a gun smuggler, always showing off about it. Bringing Frederico these fucking unbelievable weapons that Frederico just leaves lying around like chick magnets. So I just took one.

So I'm standing in the maternity ward with this Colt .45 in the gym bag. I want to make this big. And I want Jody to see. I want her to pay attention to this.

I unzip my gym bag and take the gun out. All these people start shrieking like you hear in disaster movies. High-pitched porcine squeals. Even if I wasn't a hundred percent sure about doing it, the sound of those squeals would have decided me. I wedge the black muzzle against my temple and pull the trigger.

. . .

So next thing I know, right, I'm awake. I don't remember at first. I'm just in this white room. There's tubes in my arms and a tent over my bed. But it all comes flooding back pretty quickly. And then there are dozens of doctors swarming around me. Marveling over me. The bullet traversed my prefrontal cortex and went out my right temple, but I'm fine. I'm better than I ever was, actually. They tell me I've, in effect, lobotomized myself. And I understand perfectly that this should be disastrous. I should be upset. But I'm at peace. I see more of Jody than I ever did. She's an assistant to the chief psych resident. She's my shrink. I'm her patient.

As for the *thing,* thank god, it's a boy.

Because I know, better than most, girls are trouble.

CIRCUS

When I was seven, my mother forgot my name. By the time I was twelve, I'd often have to go find her, wandering the road that led to our house. My father was busy. My brother Bill didn't care.

Sometimes Mom would wander all the way to Johnson's Pond. She'd be standing there looking at the water or, more often, repeatedly dunking her hands in the water—even though the pond was incredibly rank.

I never knew how she'd react, so I'd approach slowly, talking to her in a soft voice. "It's just me," I'd say. "It's just Joe, Mom. I'm walking up behind you now and I'm going to put my hand on your shoulder. I'm Joe, I'm your son. It's okay."

There were times when it didn't work. When she'd either get spooked and take off running or else maybe jump into the water and thrash around and it wasn't a deep pond but you can drown in very little water and so I'd go traipsing in there after her and it was never really much fun, but I cared about her, I hated her and cared about her, and really, there wasn't anything I wouldn't do to help.

It wasn't any common form of illness, and dozens of neurologists and psychiatrists were baffled and finally suggested we institutionalize her. Dad didn't want to. Not that he could deal with her or with the disease. Just that he didn't want the guilt of locking his wife away. And for the most part, she was harmless.

Then Dad died. Had a heart attack. He was only fifty-two.

My brother Bill came home from college and we dealt with everything. Bill didn't seem too shaken about Dad's death. I was sad but, more than anything, worried about Mom. We had to send her to Golden Hills.

The night before we were taking her there, I spent time with Mom in the living room. She was sitting on the velvet couch with her hands folded in her lap. She was staring ahead.

"Mom," I said, "tomorrow me and Bill are taking you to another house to live. But I'm going to come there to see you a lot, Mom, okay?"

"Who is speaking?" she said, looking in my general direction but not right at me.

"Mom, it's me. It's Joe, Mom. It's me," I said.

"Oh yes. Yes. Forgive me," she said, and it was obvious she had no idea who I was.

I was about to try leading her up to her bedroom when she stood up and walked over to the piano.

She sat down and hunched over the instrument. Her long fingers moved in a graceful blur. I don't know what she was playing. I think it just came out of her head. It was slow and sad and really the most beautiful music I'd ever heard.

• • •

When Mom died, I was in New York, going to NYU. I got a phone call from Golden Hills: We're sorry, Mr. Kitterman, your mother has passed away. It wasn't a big shock. But I wondered at fate dealing me the premature death of both parents.

I hung up the phone. I was living with my girlfriend, Maxine. She was asleep. I woke her and told her Mom was gone.

"I'm going to catch a train upstate," I told Maxine. "I'll probably stay up there a few days."

"Whatever," she said.

Maxine was cultivating nihilism that spring.

Not many people attended the funeral. Mom's brother, Henry. My brother Bill and his wife, Bliss. We buried Mom next to Dad.

When the funeral was over, I just couldn't bear to go back to New York. I just didn't feel right about it. So I decided to move into the house. Bill didn't care. He lived in Connecticut now. If I wanted to live there it was fine by him.

I called Maxine to tell her I was staying upstate. At first she screamed at me. "Joe, you can't pull shit like this, you can't just up and leave."

"I'm sorry, Max," I said. "It's just something I have to do."

"I just bet it is," she said nastily. She'd never seemed to like me beyond the first two weeks we were together. She was relieved I was leaving. Yet she thought she should put on a show of being upset. So I let her.

Eventually, she said, "Whatever, Joe, whatever," and hung up on me.

It was a little strange moving into the house. I could still feel Mom in there. Not so much Dad. Just her. Sometimes, at night, I'd think I could hear her softly playing piano. Other times I'd look out the window and mistake the moonlight for her nightgown, the long blue one that flowed out behind her.

I did some gardening and took care of the house. It was really coming apart at the seams, like it was letting itself go after my parents' deaths. I spent a lot of time doing repairs and rewiring. I figured all this stuff out from how-to books in Dad's library. He'd never done this sort of thing himself but I guess had always meant to.

There were a lot of animals around. They seemed to just gravitate to the few acres behind the house. Deer, rabbits, squirrels, some feral cats, and eventually a dog. He stuck around and I named him Pete. I don't know what kind of dog Pete was but we got along. One day, I took him to the vet for a checkup.

The vet's assistant introduced herself as Lisette. She had long brown hair in a braid down her black. She was small. She was nice looking.

"What a cutie," she said, looking down at Pete—although for some reason I thought she meant me.

"Yeah, he's a cool dog," I said, pleased. "Pete, jump up," I told my dog, extending my arms so he could leap up into them the way he would do. He wasn't a small dog but neither was he huge. About thirty-five pounds. He jumped up.

"Oh! That's darling," Lisette said, clapping her hands together like an amused child. "What else can he do?"

"Oh, geez, all kinds of stuff," I said. "Pete! Spin!" I said—at which Pete spun around in circles.

Lisette was totally enthralled with Pete. The vet, Dr. Ted, liked Pete too and talked to him sweetly as he administered shots and things.

"You've got quite a way with dogs," Lisette said when Pete had gotten all his shots and we were back in the front office, settling the bill.

"Oh, yeah, well, Pete likes me," I said.

"So does Travis," Lisette said, indicating the big old stray mutt that was living there at the vet's while they tried to find him a home. Travis was just sitting there looking at me and thumping his tail against the floor.

I ended up taking Travis home. At first Pete went into a depression about it, but eventually he got to liking Travis. He never took to Lisette, though. She and I went on a few dates and got along. She was a straightforward girl. Not particularly bright but warm. No bullshit or mood swings. Pretty soon she was spending the night a couple times a week. I didn't exactly love her, but she was nice. I think the main thing she liked about me was the way I had with dogs. Sometimes she'd sort of nag me about what was I doing just living in that house all the time, not working. I explained I had a little money from my parents' wills and I lived frugally and could make it last quite a while. She seemed to think this was stupid, though. Maybe it was.

After about six months, Lisette met someone else. I missed her. But not terribly.

Things went along fine for quite a while. I'd get up with the sun and go out in the yard and do some tai chi. Then I'd either garden or do repairs on the house. In the afternoon I worked with the dogs. I taught Travis to spin same as I'd done with Pete. They'd look like two whirling dervishes spinning like that, Travis just a blur of reddish fur and Pete a black flurry. I taught them other stuff too. To fetch, of course, but also to jump up in my arms or to jump little obstacle courses I built them. Like that.

A number of years went by. It was all fine. I'd made tiny investments with Bill's help and so I had enough money to get a new roof on the house. It disturbed me to have roofers hanging around every day for two months, but the house would have rotted away, so I had to. I stayed up in Mom's old room when the roofers were around. If they needed to ask me something, they left a note. I was glad when they were done and I didn't let anyone else come over after that. It was solitary but I liked it.

Then Pete got cancer. I refused to let him die. I put him on a special diet and took him to acupuncture for pain reduction. Then, three months into Pete's illness, Travis died. He'd been old to begin with so I'd known I wouldn't have him forever, but his dying right then was unfortunate. It made me cling to Pete a lot more, and this didn't do Pete any good. It was like I was putting emotional pressure on this very sick dog. After a few more months he was just in too much pain and I had to have him put to sleep.

Lisette didn't work at Dr. Ted's office anymore. It was some guy named James. Dr. Ted and James were very quiet as I put poor sick Pete up on the metal examining table. Dr. Ted administered the lethal injections. I saw Pete quiver a little, and then he was still.

I don't know what I did then. I walked, I guess. I walked for a long, long time. I went to Johnson's Pond. I was just on automatic really and next thing I knew, I was immersed in the pond. Like I was doing some weird baptismal rite or reenacting what Mom used to do or something. I don't know.

Then I got cold and went back to the house.

Bill found me in there about three weeks later. I wasn't in very good shape, I guess. He had come to tell me he wanted to sell the house. But finding me like that, he didn't tell me anything. He sent me to the hospital.

When I got out, I went back to New York City. After being around others in the hospital it got so I needed to see people. Just looking at all the things that played out in human faces made me feel all right and I decided I had to live in the city again.

· · ·

I had all my belongings in a shopping cart: my coat, my books, and my tools. I kept the books neatly stacked at the bottom of the cart with my coat thrown over them for protection. I stored the tools in a large wooden crate on top of the coat. I was one of the tidier guys you'd see shuffling his life before him in a cart.

Once I'd gone into the hospital, my brother Bill had taken over my share of the money from selling our parents' house. I guess he had it in an account for me, but I didn't feel like talking to him. I didn't need much money anyway. I did repairs in some of the buildings surrounding the park. The buildings' superintendents were supposed to fix things themselves but were too lazy or drunk and instead hired me. I came cheaper than any legitimate contractor.

When I wasn't doing odd jobs, I sat in the park reading. A lot of animals would come up to me. Squirrels and especially dogs—although usually they were on a leash and their humans wouldn't let them linger near me. But the squirrels would hang around, eating crumbs out of my hand and whatnot. There were also about a dozen cats that would poke about on the roof where I slept nights. When I could, I got them food. They were good company.

Occasionally someone would talk to me, but I just feigned incomprehension. Until the day the girl spoke to me.

It was early spring. I was sitting on a bench doing some reading. Suddenly a scraggly little mutt jumped up next to me on the bench, and at the same time a big Bernese Mountain Dog poked his nose in my lap.

"Treble, Minx, come on, guys," a voice says and I look up to see a lovely young woman pulling on the two dogs' leashes.

"Sorry, they've got no manners," the woman says, smiling at

me. Right away I notice this light smattering of freckles across her nose. That and the way her eyes are. Really huge eyes.

"No problem, they're great," I say, patting both the dogs.

"Oh, I love that book," the woman says now, noticing the copy of *The Loser* that I've got in my lap.

"Yes, it's a good one," I say slowly, drawing out each syllable, wishing to keep her here as long as possible.

"It's such a heartbreak, really," she says, frowning, "that guy giving his Steinway away to some kid just 'cause he can't play as well as Glenn Gould." She shakes her head and looks genuinely sad.

"Yes, it is sad." I nod.

The little mutt is in my lap now and the woman notices.

"Minx, down!" she says.

"No, let her stay, it's fine."

"They sure do like you," she says, inspecting me more closely.

"Dogs do. People not so much. But dogs, yes."

This makes her laugh. She has a wonderful laugh. It goes into her eyes and you know it's genuine.

"Nice dogs you got there," I say, patting the mutt in my lap and looking down at the Bernese.

"Not mine, I'm afraid. I'm a dog walker."

"Is that so?"

"It is, yes."

"You have a lot of dogs of your own?"

"None, actually. Cats. Three. No dogs. Not at the moment."

"That's too bad."

"Well, dogs in the city and all. I don't know. I love dogs but I don't want to keep one cooped up."

"Yes," I say, nodding my head.

"I'd better get going," she says then, looking a little worried now. "Nice talking to you."

"Likewise. See you around," I say, and she has no way of knowing how much I actually mean this, how I end up spending the next four days camped out on that very spot, hoping to see her again, how I even turn down a little plumbing job because it would interfere with my stakeout in that spot. She has no way of knowing, but at last, when I see her again, five days later, I play it cool, and this time I am reading a new Kafka translation because maybe, being a Bernhard fan, maybe she has a fixation for writers who lived in Austria and maybe this will lure her in and give me time to think of other things to bring into the conversation. Even though I've had five days to plan this conversation, I know that once I see her again, once I see that shoulder-length straw-colored hair and that smattering of freckles, all sense will leave my head. I haven't even thought about women since Lisette and that was three years ago now, and occasionally women have looked at me, even in my current state as guy with a shopping cart, because I guess I still look remotely all right, and sometimes cute squatter girls or batty old women and once even a tough-looking woman in a business suit have looked at me, but these looks did nothing for me. It is her look that I want. Hers, although I don't know her name, and at least I have to get that much out of her, at least the name.

And then she is there, with the same two dogs, these dogs recognizing me long before she does and pulling her over to me.

"Oh, hello," she says. "I guess they've missed you." She laughs, trying to rein the dogs back in.

"What's your name?" I blurt out at once, this catching her by surprise and that little frown of hers creasing her brow.

"Katie Murphy," she says, looking at me a little strangely. "And you?" she adds then—although just out of politeness, for I can see she is spooked that I've asked her name.

"Joe. Joe Kitterman."

"Well, Joe Kitterman, it's nice to make your acquaintance," she says now, extending her free hand while the other mans the dogs' leashes.

"Oh, those stories," Katie says, noticing the Kafka tome in my lap.

"Yes," I say, and it has worked, my plan has worked, for she so wants to discuss *In the Penal Colony* that she sits down next to me on the bench. There is no hesitation, just a fervor over *In the Penal Colony*, and soon we are talking, we are talking as people do, not stuttering and monosyllabic the way I thought I'd be, no, not at all, there is flow, there is motion, there is light.

After some time she stuns me by asking if I'd like to get a cup of coffee together. She has to return the dogs first, but then she'll come back for me. Will I still be in the same spot, she asks.

"I'm homeless," I say then, not intending to but it somehow spilling out of me.

"Yes. Well. Some people are," she says after a pause.

"What I mean is, I'm not going anywhere. Take the dogs back. I'll be here."

"Okay, then," she says, tugging on the dogs, and Minx, the little mutt, puts up a big struggle.

"Go on, now, get going, go home," I tell the dog, and she looks up at me with her little dog eyes and then goes.

Soon Katie and I are sitting in Odessa, in the back, where smoking is permitted, for Katie smokes like crazy.

"It's awful, I just can't keep them out of my mouth," she says now, reaching for the fourth cigarette in ten minutes.

"Oh?" I say.

"My father died last month and predictably I've been smoking a lot and even drinking and I never usually drink."

"I'm sorry."

"So am I. My lungs hurt."

And I ask about her father and she tells me, an unusual man, a lion tamer who raised her in the circus, and whenever she'd see her mother or her kid sister, neither of whom had ever wholly approved of circus life, Katie would feel odd and freakish, but she never fit in at the circus either and so moved to New York and didn't look back, and now she wishes she had, wishes she'd seen more of her father before the heart attack took him, and as she says this, I watch her smoke and I think of her lungs, situated there beneath her small chest. For a brief second I let my eyes pass over this chest and it is becoming increasingly difficult not to stare at all parts of her, not to commit everything to memory, and then, for some reason, I start telling her far more than I'd intended, about those years living in the house, about Pete and Travis and about Mom's music that I kept on hearing long after her death.

"I'd be lying in bed some nights and the dogs would be there all curled up on the little beds I'd made them and then suddenly it would come, this sort of wave of music, soft at first and then insistent, like it was trying to tell me something," I say, and immediately feel like a crackpot.

"I did have a breakdown, you know," I tell her. "I was off in a hospital for a while, but I'm not a nut, I'm really not," I tell her, and this makes her laugh, that same beautiful laugh that goes into her eyes and lights them up.

• • •

When we've been there two hours and it's evident that we've a great deal to say to each other, she asks do I want to go to the movies tomorrow, and this startles me. I never expected that it would work, this ruse of mine of just listening to her, of offering myself to her on a subconscious level, offering all I have in me, intuiting that she'd never gotten this from someone, that no one had wholly, and in just the space of one afternoon, put themselves at her mercy, intuiting that this would get her attention and that all the things in my head could perhaps come to fruition. I hadn't expected it to work but now it has and we agree to meet, and then she is off. I watch her walk up the avenue and I return to the park, where I've left my shopping cart under the supervision of Dishboy, the crazy kid whose squat burned down, and Dishboy is stoned and just sitting, staring at his shoes, and my cart is there intact.

"Thanks, Dishboy," I tell him and I give him a dollar and then wheel my cart to the other side of the park. I sit down and spend quite a while just staring at my shopping cart. After some time, I pick out a few of my books and my ancient suit and then I just walk away, leaving the cart and the tools behind.

I wander out of the park and west, walking down Ninth Street, just looking at things and people. I have a new freedom now that I've relinquished my cart, but no sooner have I appreciated this fact than I begin to worry and even shake a bit, for how do I know anything will ever be any different, how do I know I will find a way to scrape by without doing odd jobs for supers, and now my hands are shaking terribly and to stop them I quickly head back into the park and dunk my hands in the little pool of water that has built up in the drinking fountain, the drain of which is clogged with gum.

It would be better if I immersed my whole body. But the hands or feet will do, and now, yes, I feel myself growing calmer, and after a few moments I walk to the other side of the park and it is beautiful out, dozens of mothers and kids and bums and psychos and skate punks are all abounding, vivid in their spring faces and clothes, and although a few hours ago this sight depressed me, now I feel fine about these many great gashes of color and I head east and south, down Bowery right past Rivington Street.

I go up the newly painted red steps to the Andrew Hotel, which is one of the less popular flophouses. I give the guy with the veined nose my six dollars. He opens the gate to let me in, then steers me back into one of the chicken-wire-enclosed rooms, where I sit down on the bed and think.

After a while, I go back outside, to the bodega on Prince Street. The guy in here knows me, has a knack for memorizing the many faces that appear before him, and although I'm not that frequent a patron of the flophouse or of this bodega, he gives me a warm smile of recognition and helps me select the least expensive toothbrush, disposable razor, and soap. The total is a mere dollar and thirty-nine cents and I am grateful for this and for this man who remembers my face.

I return to the hotel and to my bed, and although the place is getting full now and there is noise, what with the TV and guys with DTs making strange sounds, I lay down and slip off into sleep.

When I wake up it's dawn and I go into the decrepit communal shower and begin to bathe fastidiously. I scrub every inch of myself and brush my teeth thoroughly. I shave. I comb through my hair that is still dark brown without gray. I stand for some time looking at myself in the mirror, which is a thing I haven't done in many months, and there are such crevices in my face, as if someone had cut valleys in me, but I am still here, Joe, looking as I do, which isn't so bad, which used to cause many women to talk to me, and now there is Katie, and she has talked to me, and now it is only 7 A.M. but I am ready, I am clean and I am ready.

We're on her bed but I'm frozen, and when she holds me I tremble and at last tell her about the water. About the habit I've gotten into of dunking my hands in water to soothe myself.

"Well, Joe, I've got water here," she says, taking my hand and pulling me up off the bed and into the bathroom, and soon a great gush of water is pouring into the tub and she is removing all her clothes, revealing her blessed body to me, small but broad in the shoulders and hips, then tiny in the waist.

"Come on, Joe," she says and she starts peeling off my clothes as I am just standing there.

And now we are in the tub with the warm water still gushing in and we are standing with the water rushing around our calves. "Is this calming you?" she asks and at last, yes, I feel calmed and I nod, and then the deep freeze I've been in starts to melt and I put my hands on her shoulders and lean over and softly kiss her, her mouth immediately yielding and blooming, and I am transformed at once, I am new, and I wrap my whole body around hers. I hold her within, deeply within me, and it is not until the water begins overflowing that she gently pulls away and turns off the tap and then leads me back out of the bathroom, and we patter gently, our wet feet slapping the dirty floor as we go back into the main room and onto the bed, and one of her cats is there on the bed but now promptly jumps off and I say "Katie" in a soft voice and cover her with my body.

I never meant to leave Katie. I'd told her I never would and she'd looked at me with those large eyes so green. "I know you mean that, Joe," she'd said. Although I had never gone back for my shopping cart, I continued sleeping on the roof on

Avenue C. I got a part-time job at the Strand Book Store and could have afforded a room or moved in with Katie, for she had asked, "Joe, do you want to live here with me?" And it made me sad to know that I couldn't, that although Katie's body and love and kindness had picked me up from a dark place, I couldn't go so far as to share the day-to-day exigencies of life with her, and I wanted to hurt myself for the pain I gave her but it couldn't be helped. I had somehow misled her. The whole reason she'd fallen for me had to do with unspoken promises and offerings, and now these were empty. And so Katie had started pulling away from me. It was subtle, as were most of the things we did, but we were so keenly in tune with each other, there was no way not to feel it. She was protecting herself. She was taking parts of herself and hiding them from me.

And then came the day of the circus. I had never been. Mom was always too ill and Dad too busy. I only knew about circuses, but I'd never experienced one.

I came over to Katie's place early. We had both, independently of each other, decided to really dress up for the occasion—although even I knew no one dresses up for the circus anymore.

Katie was lovely in a blue dress and I had had my suit dry-cleaned, but now I noticed there were loose threads hanging off it.

"I need to shave my suit," I said after kissing her hello.

"What?" she asked, her eyes getting bigger the way they would when something was strange or funny.

"It's the only way to make it presentable," I said, then explained about shaving off the stray threads.

We went into the bathroom, where she found a Bic shaver. She stood watching as I shaved my suit. She laughed at me for this, but the loose threads came away and the suit looked nicer.

We walked over to Madison Square Garden. It wasn't far from where Katie lived.

There were people selling circus baubles. Flashlights and stuffed lions and cups with clown faces on them.

There were kids everywhere. Often the parents were not much older than their kids. They were people with hard lives, and these showed in their faces and in their odd cheap clothes.

Katie bought us a big box of Cracker Jacks and, as we took our seats, burrowed in looking for the prize before even eating a single Cracker Jack.

"Katie, I do love you," I said as she pulled out the prize, a little tattoo of Tom and Jerry.

She licked the tattoo, then applied it to my hand.

"I know, Joe," she said as the the house lights dimmed and the circus started up. A bunch of elephants came trundling into the main ring as three acrobats took to the high wires above. My heart started pumping hard in my chest. There was a giant and a midget and then, of course, more animals: tigers and ponies and dogs. Poodles and terriers and some other kinds of big dogs, and the big dogs jumped through hoops and the poodles rode skateboards and my heart ached for the dogs.

When intermission came, I looked down at my hand and the Tom and Jerry tattoo was all smeared, and I reached my arm around Katie's shoulders and felt her recoil slightly.

"What's the matter?" I asked.

"Nothing. I'm just tired."

"Something's wrong."

"Why does anything have to be wrong?"

"It doesn't, but something is."

"When are you going to stop living on the streets, Joe? I mean, there's no reason for it. None at all. You have money now," she said, blurting it out fast, like it'd been at the tip of her tongue for a long time.

I felt so bad.

"I thought you understood it," I said.

"I did, Joe, at first. I understood you'd been through some weird things and needed to live this sort of extreme life to get over it. Now, though, you should be all right. You should think about getting an apartment. I offered you to move in. I don't know why you didn't want to."

"The offer doesn't stand anymore, does it?" I said, looking into those strange green eyes of hers.

"Oh, don't say that, Joe," she said, and the way her face looked was something I'll never forget.

"Well, it doesn't, does it?" I persisted.

"Oh," she sighed, "I guess not, Joe. I guess not."

I took her hand in mine and squeezed it hard, but I knew this couldn't help at all.

When the circus started back up, my heart pumped fast again. I was alive like I'd never been. Not even Katie could do to me what this was doing to me.

When the show was over, Katie led me downstairs to the backstage entrance, where the lion tamer, a friend of her late father's, had left her name on the backstage guest list.

We walked into the cool entrails of the place. There was so much activity. Clowns taking off parts of their costumes, roadies in sleek black clothing. We were walking around a curve, back toward where the lion cages were, when I stopped short at the dogs.

One of the dog trainers was there, a woman in a blue sequined suit.

"I just need to look at the dogs for a minute," I told Katie.

"Okay. I'll be over there." She shrugged and pointed to the lion cages.

• • •

I didn't even make it there, though. The woman in the blue se-quined suit was having difficulty getting one of the big dogs to cooperate. I took a few steps toward the dog and started talking to him. After a few seconds, he went right into his cage.

"Hey, what'd you say to him?" the woman asked me.

"Nothing much," I said.

I guess she liked the way I talked about dogs and to the dogs. Her name was Sarah. We got to talking and pretty soon she told me she could use an assistant. Not much pay, but I'd have a place to sleep. And I'd be with dogs. Every day.

I went to find Katie near the lions. She was talking to the lion tamer. He had bleached blonde hair. He had one arm around Katie's shoulder. Even so, I could tell she didn't belong at the circus. Not really. Not the way I do.

I walked Katie home and I told her about my job offer and one tear came to her eye.

"Oh, Joe," she said, "you suck."

"I do?"

"Joe," she said, then looked down and added, "I'm glad you found your place. But you suck."

"I'm sorry."

"So am I," she said.

I went upstairs with her. I collected the few things I had there. A toothbrush. A shirt. A few books. After that, when I had my arms full of stuff and was just looking at her, she patted my cheek and said "Bye" and then let me out the door.

When I got outside, I just stood there for a long time. On Fortieth Street. I stood there until I knew she'd be all right. And maybe it's what everyone thinks when they run away from someone, but I truly felt that some other man would come along. A man who would want the things she wants. Who could always hold her the way I used to, with abandon and contentment at once.

I went down to my roof to organize the few things I had there, stashed in various crevices.

I put my books and my clothes into a plastic bag.

I caught the bus up to the Garden.

Sarah, my new boss, had already crated up all the dogs and was just getting into the back of the truck.

"I was starting to wonder about you. I was about to leave without you," Sarah said. She had her fists bunched up on her hips. "I'm glad you made it. You can take the top bunk," she told me, gesturing into the back of the truck, above the dog crates, where there were two bunks. I nodded and climbed in. The dogs were mostly quiet, settling in for the ride. It smelled strongly of wet dog. It was stifling. But soothing.

"Put your stuff there for now," Sarah told me, motioning to an empty crate. "I'm gonna get some sleep, I'm dead," she told me. "Simon, the guy driving the truck, he'll wake us up when we get into Philadelphia," she said as she climbed up into her bunk.

"Okay," I said. I put my stuff into the empty crate and climbed up to my own bunk. It was narrow, almost like a coffin. I lay down and pulled the thin blanket over myself. I felt more comfortable than I had in years.

TEETH

Sometimes I can't believe the shit that comes out of my teeth. When I'm flossing I mean. Huge helpings of white gunk. Amazing that that kind of thing can be in there, in my own goddamned mouth, and I don't even know about it.

It's hard to get through the day sometimes thinking about stuff like that. About the precariousness of it all. What holds it together. How my brain tells my finger to wind the floss around my other finger and go saw down the paste in my mouth. Or how those neurons swim around, sparking one another like dogs in heat, sending millions of messages per minute all just to tell my left eyelid to blink for godsakes. Imagine that kind of frenzied activity for the sake of a goddamned *blink?* It's ridiculous. It's precarious. It makes me want to wear some protection. A helmet. Steel reinforcement. Padding. The whole bit.

Shit could just fall on your head, you know. And slice into

your goddamned brain. Like INVOLUNTARY HEMI-SPHERECTOMY. You could just be poking along, going to your asswipe job, where Christina, the intern from Harvard, will be there, kitted up in god knows what, and you're supposed to walk around not getting a hard-on when actually the breath of life itself tends to give you a hard-on because you've pulled through a lot of shit in your thirty-one years, and sometimes it's so bright, the very fact of your surviving, it's so bright and huge, it gives you a hard-on, and if that can do it, well, you'd better believe Christina can do it, and you're poking along, walking across Eighteenth Street to *the abomination,* as you like to call your job, and WHAMO, right, some disgruntled fuck on a construction scaffolding is like, fuck this, man, and he just lets one loose, right, like one of those immense bricklaying SCALPELS those guys have, he's like, fuck it, and fuck that guy walking down the street, and BAM, he sends that thing flying down and it goes in your head, blade first, and plants in your brain, slicing apart your two hemispheres, like your head's a fucking birthday cake. Right?

I mean, that happens. And it's a marvel really that we're here. Life is a gift.

So anyway. I'm thinking about this stuff.

Then some things happen. Some bad things. And I'm thinking about it a little too much. About the gunk in my teeth. About wearing a helmet. What have you.

So I go in to see the shrink. And I let her have it. She's always cooing at me how she wants to hear everything, *whatever comes into your mind, Jack,* so I tell her everything. I'm like, "Doctor Ray, I mean Jody"—because yeah, my shrink wants me to be on first-name basis with her, which maybe has to do with her still being a *student shrink* that I got through some discount shrink referral place—but although I call her Jody, and although it's a nice, even provocative, name, she's a very plain, girl who's always giving you the eye, and ain't it your luck that the girl giving you the eye happens to have *pink eyes,* right? So your lungs, they're really taking a beating from all this, they're incredibly busy in there, and then there's the old windpipe that, you think, maybe one day somebody's gonna pierce a hole in and give you a tracheotomy when you've smoked yourself into lung cancer, emphysema, or some newfangled smoker's Ebola that you will inevitably contract now that you've been fired from your suckass job because one day, you are standing waiting for the elevator, and Christina the Harvard intern is looking like a whore from central casting and has this *vinyl miniskirt* on, and librarian glasses sliding down her nose into her ridiculously perfect toothy smile, and you can trust there's no gunk in *those* teeth, no filmy goop on *that* smile that just adds a little more to the trendy look of her that is so tired you can't believe it's giving you a hard-on, because, in spite of having grown up rough and broke, you're an AESTHETE, man, you've been to Rome, you've wept at the majesty of Caravaggio and gawked up at the fucking SISTINE CHAPEL, and how the fuck did that guy *do that,* and god, you are just a puny exploited sack of shit compared to ROME, man, and in spite of all this, in spite of your appreciation for, your deep understanding of beauty, this little Harvard intern in a predictable miniskirt with seamed stockings, she's getting you hot just looking at her, all of which is just further evidence of your fucked-up neuroanatomy—that its wiring should permit an aesthetic lapse like this—but before you have time to dwell on this, the elevator comes and all the slobs from the executive floor are packed on, pressing you close to the intern, and as you look down at the top of her shiny intern head, she looks up and smiles at you, a blinding smile that makes your eyes hurt, and then—and this is almost worse than some construction fuck dropping a scalpel on your head, right—then she rubs her ass into your crotch, I SHIT YOU

NOT, rubs her ass into your crotch in that packed elevator full of suits and Calvin Klein cologne, the scent of which you recognize because once you had a go with a gay guy who rammed it up your ass because you wanted to experience the other end of sexuality, as it were, and you saw him dousing himself in Calvin Klein cologne right before he bent you over his expensive four-poster bed with chains fitted onto two of the posters and rammed himself up your ass, and thereafter you permanently associated the scent of Calvin Klein with *ass fucking*, which is probably exactly what you're supposed to do, and so the elevator stinks of ass fucking, and Christina the intern all the sudden grinds that vinyl-clad ass of hers into your worn-down corduroy pants, giving you the most instantaneous and hard-core hard-on, and when she gets off on the second floor—instead of going all the way to the lobby like everyone else—you get off too, leaving all the suits and the secretaries behind, and you follow her into the disused ladies' room and find her planted there before the mirror, examining herself, her eyes grasping lovingly at the reflection as she runs her hands down her sides in a smoothing gesture, as if there were great waves of unrest there beneath her clothes, and then her eyes meet yours in the mirror and she gives you a slow smile but says nothing and, mesmerized and horrified at once, you come up behind her and, not breaking eye contact with her in the mirror, hike her skirt up over her ass. She bends forward a little to facilitate the process as you grind your still-clothed crotch into her, causing a thrust of her hips and a little gasping sound, and as her head lolls loose, those big ridiculous black-rimmed glasses slide down her nose and, infuriated by these eyeglasses, by their statement of deliberate homeliness, you push her shoulders and bend her forward over the sink and rip the stockings and panties down over her ass, and now suddenly her asshole is confronting you, it is winking at you, pink and surrounded in a great many black hairs, which somehow you hadn't expected, and not that you were going to fuck her in the ass anyway, but the sight of her asshole, surrounded as it is with that tremendous beard of hair, it turns your stomach, it horrifies you so much it swells you so big; your dick would go up her intestines and pop out her mouth, but this moment of horror, although it's made you harder, it also tempers the whole thing, and for a moment you flash on Caravaggio, specifically on *The Lute Player,* one of the Caravaggios at the Met, as it's one of the few Caravaggios you've seen lately, and in spite of it being a lesser painting, you still wanted it, you wanted it more than you've wanted anything, and so you went up to it, the Met was crowded, you went up and touched the Caravaggio expecting to set off alarms or maybe a spray of tear gas that would rain down on you from the fire extinguisher, or at the very least the security guard would escort you out of the Met, but fucking NOTHING HAPPENED, you touched the Caravaggio long enough to have potentially sliced it out of its frame and stuffed it down your pants and walked out of there, and nothing happened when you touched it—except of course you got a hard-on, more formidable even than the one the sight of Christina's Brilloed butthole gives you, and Christina can't hold a candle to Caravaggio, and although it is not necessarily wise to hold your sexual encounters up to the standards of Baroque Italian painting, for some reason, in this moment, you do, and you just back off from the little intern bitch, she's waiting, she's beating like a heart in an open chest wound, but you back off and, saying not one word, turn around back out of that bathroom, and next thing you know, you're called into Personnel and not only fired but slapped with attempted rape charges, and now you've got no health insurance, and so when you do at last contract smoker's Ebola, you will be relegated to Bellevue and will probably die of TB contracted from some skinless fuck they fished out of the East River."

. . .

So the thing of it is, the day I tell all this to my shrink, Jody, it starts with my teeth. With the gunk in my teeth. Which, as I've mentioned, makes Jody laugh. I then go on to explain how precarious I feel life is and what will I do if I contract a fatal disease since I've been fired and thus have no health insurance.

Now, the bit about my getting fired, that comes right in the middle of my whole diatribe about my lungs and my liver. I just launch right into the whole story about the intern trying to get me to fuck her in the bathroom. So, right when I'm telling Jody about the intern's Brillo pad asshole winking at me, I turn around, right. Because I lie on the couch, because Jody, although a psychiatrist, is in the experimental phase of her training, where she's trying out some of that Freudian stuff, and so I lie supine on the couch with my back to her and it occurs to me then that although I am accustomed to detailing for her my sexual liaisons, I've never told her something quite this relentlessly hateful, and so all the sudden, I prop up on my elbow and look back to see how Jody's taking all this because she hasn't said a word, or even grunted, in several long minutes.

And don't you know, Jody, my button-down yellow and navy Upper East Side student shrink, is jerking off. I kid you not.

I did not want to believe this. It just wasn't possible. My shrink jerking off while I'm spilling my guts. But she was. She had her hand foisted down her skirt, moving down there, touching herself under there.

Talk about inappropriate behavior.

She rips her hand out of there, which is the giveaway. Maybe if she just gently, and with some embarrassment, removed her hand from her skirt, maybe I'd attribute all this to crotch rot. She just had to scratch herself. But the way she pulls her hand out, well, there's only one way to interpret it.

I stare at her and she stares back.

Her red hair is lustrous. She's wearing a tasteful shade of lipstick. She'd fit in as the racier element in a corporate boardroom. Or maybe as a tough-as-nails but slightly sexy criminal prosecutor. Like that. Not the sort of woman you imagine jerking off to your pathetic story of sexual depravity in the corporate world. Not the kind of woman you imagine FUCKING HERSELF as you pour out the wasteland of your id.

I feel rage tighten up my veins. I stand up. I can't speak. I can't move. I want to throw furniture. I want to crack her skull open with a chair. Because in that instant, I know. I know she's been jerking herself off all along. Like when I told her about my one-night stand with the girl from the A.A. meetings. She touched herself over that one and she probably fingered herself so hard she scabbed over when I told her about the gay guy ramming it up my ass. And I can only guess how violently she came over my prolonged affair with the Mormon girl who wouldn't fuck me but would blow me obsessively, like everywhere, like the more public the better.

I just stare at Jody. And she stares right back. Her eyes are the palest blue. She clears her throat. "Ahem," she says, and once she's cleared her throat, she pulls it together. She's going to pretend this has never happened.

"Not so easy, Jody," I say to her then, and my heart is racing. "What were you doing just now?" I ask her, my voice a whisper as I take a step closer to her and feel how I'm getting a hard-on over the notion of talking to my shrink like this. I am breaking down all the barriers. I am pushing the envelope. Me. Jack. Jack, who's grown so quiet. So respectable since he quit drinking. Jack is back.

"I was listening to you, Jack," Jody says then.

"You were touching yourself," I say, taking another step toward her, not sure if I'm going to strangle her or fuck her, and she's still poised, she's got her sheathed-in-flesh-color-stockinged legs crossed demurely at the ankles. And then she actually says: "AND HOW DOES THAT MAKE YOU FEEL, JACK?"

I don't know if I should laugh or scream, and so I actually take a moment to reflect on exactly how this does make me feel, but all I can think of are my berserk neurons, sparking and sputtering like a million cheap firecrackers in Chinatown, and then, reflexively, I kneel before Jody. "This is how it makes me feel, Jody," I say, looking up into those pale blue eyes that still fail to register emotion of any kind.

I stick my hand up that midcalf navy skirt and I'm expecting the double obstructions of Bloomingdale's reinforced-crotch pantyhose and Jockey For Her briefs, but she's got NOTHING ON UNDER THERE. My shrink is wearing flesh-colored thigh-high stockings and THAT'S IT, and I'm just baffled. I mean, stuff like this just doesn't happen to me, and yet here it is, and here *she* is, and my fingers go right in her and she goes nuts. She thrusts out her hips and lets loose this moan like you wouldn't believe. And I'm totally fucking appalled. I mean, this lady's supposed to be straightening my life out, not begging to suck my cock as she slides down from her shrink chair, wiggles next to me, and starts ripping at my corduroys like there's heroin in there and she's a strung-out lab rat.

So I let her blow me.

Once she had emptied me and was pulling her skirt back down and wiping her mouth, she said she'd have to stop seeing me as a client but was it okay to call me for a date. I laughed at her, but this, like everything else, had no effect on her. Her face remained a mask. So I said, "I guess so," then walked out of there.

There was a nice little old lady in the waiting room and I wondered what Jody was going to do to her.

I went home and got really fucking depressed. So depressed I couldn't even obsess over the gunk in my teeth or falling victim to involuntary hemispherectomy. I mean, where the hell was I supposed to turn. All this shit I'd tried, like, when I quit drinking I went to A.A. for a while but right away this crazy girl Laura with a big red mouth with double-D-cup breasts took me to coffee and cooed twelve-step inanities at me, then took me home and fucked me, then never wanted to see me again and caused big scenes when I turned up at the A.A. meetings she went to. So I kind of lost faith in all that. But I stayed off the booze, and after being this thief and scammer most of my life, I went and got a menial clerk job at a law firm. Of course, then the thing happened with the Harvard intern and I got fired.

And now my shrink just wants to blow me.

What the fuck.

So I keep seeing Jody. I mean, she's an amazing lay and she's really smart too. Yet the thing that gets to me is this broken part of her. This thing she keeps hidden but I see once in a while when I wake up in the middle of the night and find her staring at me—not in that usual hard way, but with this tenderness. That she promptly masks. But not before it's given me hope that one day she'll calm the fuck down and stop being such a freak.

Jody lives not, as I'd always figured, on the Upper East Side, but in Tribeca, in this run-down loft with dirty white walls and nothing in it except a bed, a hideous red leather couch, and two stuffed deer heads that I refuse to ask about. Of course, Jody's seldom there since she's got hospital rounds to do at the psych ward and patients to see through the discount shrink referral place—all of which is a problem because she wants to be fucked constantly, and I end up having to meet her to fuck her in this little utility room adjoining the New York Hospital cafeteria just so she can make it through rounds. Sometimes I stop by her loft on my way back from seeing the public defender over the case with the intern, because one of the few times Jody is home is 2 P.M. I come by and, as she's given me keys, I just let myself in and can usually find her lying on the bed, studying hard with a dildo in every orifice. I swear to god. She even BLOWS dildos, she's gotta be plugged up from all ends. She's just nuts, you know. And I fall for her more and more. And I guess she likes me. I don't really know why. I'm totally broke, shoplifting to get by because now, with all this crap pending, I can't even get a lousy job, so I'm going to school up at John Jay College of Criminal Justice, taking all these criminal psychology classes, which I excel at because in spite of just being a petty thief and scammer, I guess I have a decent criminal mind, and it turns Jody on that I can discourse about the *criminal mind*, about the collector habits of serial killers or the statistics on patricide in New York City in 1962, and there's almost nothing I can do that *doesn't* turn Jody on, and for that reason alone I'd put up with almost any deranged behavior on her part.

Nearly a year goes by like this. It's the longest relationship I've had since I was seventeen. It's a total rollercoaster and I periodically start thinking about how Jody is supposed to be a *mental health professional* but was jerking off while I bared myself to her, and although she swears that was a once-in-a-lifetime occurrence, that only I and my problems rendered her a quivering sack of lust, I have my doubts. But by now I love her and I just go along, quieting my doubts, eking by.

One day, I take Jody to the Met and show her how you can touch the Caravaggios and nothing happens. We touch *The Musicians* and then *The Lute Player.* Each several times. And it gets Jody as hot as it gets me. She grabs my cock right there, in plain fucking daylight, in the Met, and then leads me downstairs to where they have all the thirteenth-century religious icon rooms, and there's couches you're allowed to sit on but you're not supposed to FUCK ON THEM, but we do, she just plops on my lap and, as ever, isn't wearing any underwear and I fuck her in front of the thirteenth-century icons. Until the security guard comes in. Because I guess they don't care if you fondle the Caravaggios but you're not supposed to fuck in front of the thirteenth-century icons. So we get kicked out of there, but Jody's so revved up over the whole thing she wants us to do something extra special: she wants us to go get a whore. I've never done it with a whore but Jody has. Naturally. I make a face but I'm intrigued nonetheless, and we go cruise Twelfth Street for a whore—not that I want to put my dick in there, but Jody wants to like, *do stuff* to the whore and have me watch. So we're walking up and down Twelfth Street and there are just a couple of incredibly skanky girls, malformed girls with limps and weird pockets of fat sticking out of their whore costumes, and Jody's about to snap, I can see it, she's gotta come and she's gotta come soon. Then we notice this sort of remotely attractive petite girl, and the thing that really makes me look twice is the miniskirt. I know I've seen that skirt before. I've seen that skirt on Christina the Harvard intern. I feel a chill go down my back. I inspect her more closely and it's gotta be her, I swear, it looks just like her. Meanwhile, Jody's totally honed in on the girl and we march up to her and Jody says, "How much?" And the whore says, "What, I do both of you?" And Jody says, "No, I do *you*." And the whore wrinkles up her nose, like she's got some weird *whore ethics* or something, and she's shaking her head no and just walks away from us.

Now Jody's fuming. She stomps her stiletto on the pavement and fucking cracks off the heel of her four-hundred-dollar shoe, and I say, "Jody, that's her. That's the little intern bitch that accused me of attempted rape." And Jody says, "Oh, Jack, don't start with me with that," because she had to hear all about it for so long—even though half the time she was being paid to—and eventually, pretty mysteriously, the whole legal thing got dropped and I never knew why. Until now.

And I say, "I'm not kidding, Jody. I know it, that's her."

So then Jody catches up with the whore and somehow strikes a deal with her. She must have offered her an insane amount of cash, I don't know. And we take the whore back to Tribeca and Jody makes her take a bath.

When the whore emerges, she's all cleaned up, almost Ivy League looking, only she smiles then and her teeth are all fucked up. Just these nasty stubby diseased teeth. It would just be medically impossible for someone's teeth to degenerate that badly in the course of a year, and so I realize it actually isn't Christina the Harvard intern but a dead ringer for her—save the teeth, of course. So then Jody gets busy with the whore, ramming stuff into her, a few dildos and some half-rotten carrots that were in the fridge. I'm jerking off, just for good measure, and because Jody's egging me on to as well.

Then we have a bad moment. All this time, I guess Jody still thinks the whore really is Christina the intern, and now Jody starts egging me on to fuck Christina, how I must do this for my own emotional growth. I'm not kidding, she turns and stage-whispers, "DO IT FOR YOUR WELL-BEING, JACK," while the whore just lies there and I try explaining how, no, this actually isn't Christina, just a dead ringer. Jody starts getting incredibly snippy with me. "Oh, fuck it, Jack," she tells me. "I don't care if it's not really her. You've got to fuck her," she says, going on further about how this intercrural atrocity will bring everything full circle and resolve things for me emotionally. Like some sort of hideous psychosexual karmic wheel or something. And the whore, who between being fucked all over her body and pumped full of downers that Jody has on hand, is totally out of it and doesn't understand what we're talking about, is, like, reaching for me, wanting a real dick in her I guess after all those marital aids. But I'm not having any part of it. I'm just not going there. I got enough problems without hooker diseases that'll make my dick fall off.

This ended up being a big point of contention with Jody. After she'd sent the Christina look-alike packing and was getting dressed to go on rounds at the hospital, Jody kept saying that she'd tried everything with me and now fate had brought us this beautiful twist, this potential *resolution* to all my problems, and I wouldn't do it. I was supposed to fuck the whore who resembled the intern bitch, and that would have solved everything. I hadn't realized there was a problem to begin with, so I didn't know what the fuck she was talking about. I guess I almost never did. And now, since I had, in Jody's mind, been contrary one too many times, Jody dismissed me. Just as she had dismissed me as her patient, I was now dismissed as her boyfriend. She got that iciness in her pale blue eyes. Her face became that same clammy mask it had been back before we'd gotten intimate. I could see she had flipped off some switch inside herself and there was no going back. So I didn't beg. I didn't grovel. I didn't shout or throw a couch. I said "Bye," then turned and walked out of there.

I went home, to East Broadway, to my creepy building next to the methadone clinic. There were a couple of really scraggly methadonians loitering on my stoop, and one of them had this box in her lap. I look in and there's this kitten. This tiny starved kitten mewing helplessly.

So I say, "What's the deal? What's with the kitten?" And the girl says she rescued it from some shooting gallery, do I want it?

So I say, "Yeah, I do."

And I take the kitten up to my tiny cramped apartment and feed it some milk and name it Kitten.

Sometimes Kitten nibbles on my finger. And she's got these tiny, perfect little teeth. Without any kind of gunk in them.

THE MESSENGER

I'm starting to get a complex. Everywhere I go, I end up solving some kind of problem. I'm not kidding. It's getting to be a burden.

Just the other day, it happened again.

I'm delivering a rush that Number Eleven was supposed to drop an hour earlier, only he got doored and landed on his face. I had to go find him at the hospital, get all his packages, and rush that one package over to Park Avenue. It's pouring rain and that fucking Weather Channel, I should sue their asses because they absolutely did not predict this and don't they know there are bike messengers like me who like LIVE for weather and for being prepared, and had I known, had the Weather Channel had its SHIT together, I would have put on that cool new blue rain suit Alfie gave me for my birthday, and I've only slept with the girl twice, she's the lone female bike messenger at the place, really a beautiful, sweet, girl, and I was really surprised and touched that she gave me a present, but it's not like I'm ever going to get to use it what with those Weather Channel fucks being dumber than a box of hair.

So I'm totally drenched and my brakes aren't working well and I get to Park Avenue to deliver Number Eleven's rush. I'm just supposed to leave it with the doorman but he tells me no, I've got to go up and deliver it in person, to the lady it's addressed to, one Lydia Hall. I'm quite backed up what with Number Eleven's packages and my own and I try to wrangle out of it, but the doorman's insistent in that icy snotty way some of these doormen have, like they're above you because they happen to work indoors, and Mr. Mortimer here implies that there will be hell to pay, and besides, I know Lydia Hall is a steady good client, and so I go up there.

"Oh, thank god you're here," she says, opening the door, and she's got on this slinky ankle-length dressing gown thing and copper-colored hair piled up on top of her head and is beautiful in that sort of nervous rich way. I hand her the package.

"If you could wait just a moment," she says, resting her hand on my arm to keep me there, as if this light touch on my arm will certainly keep me there, and I've got to hand it to her, it does, for a second.

"I'm really backed up, ma'am," I tell her. "I've got to get going. I'm sorry," I say.

"I just need to look through some things here," she says, patting the package I've delivered, "then I'll give you a return package. It'll just take a few minutes," she says. "Have a seat. Can I get you a beverage?"

"I don't mean to be rude, ma'am, but there wasn't an order for a round trip and I really have to get going."

"What's your name?" she asks, looking me up and down.

"My name is Indio."

"Indio? Well, Indio, I'll call your dispatcher to say I need you just a moment longer. How's that?"

"That's fine, only he's gonna tell you I gotta go. One of the other messengers got doored and I've got all his packages plus my own."

"I'm sorry. Only two minutes, Indio."

"Ma'am, I really have to go."

"I'm dialing," she says, picking up this antique-looking phone. "The number?" she asks me and I tell her the number at the office, and she calls in and I guess gets an earful when she tells Mikey the dispatcher she's gotta keep me here a few minutes. But then I hear her tell Mikey—in the way someone in the ruling class tells someone working class—that she's a valuable customer and requires my services a moment longer, and then she hangs up and, urging me to sit on this amazing-looking straight-backed chair there in the hallway, slips through a door into one of the rooms off the hallway.

For a second I wonder what the rest of this place looks like, and if the hallway's any gauge at all, it must be a fucking palace in here, and Lydia Hall most definitely looks like a princess, and then, as I'm standing there tapping my foot, too anxious to sit like she offered, I hear this scream coming from the room she went into and then I hear her voice say, "Help," and so of course I go in there, into the room her voice is coming from.

Lydia Hall's got her hands clutching her face and blood is pouring out between her fingers, and now she sort of flops forward, landing face first on the floor, and you know what I think right away, I just think about all that blood staining the amazing champagne-colored carpeting, and then I get down on my knees thinking, FUCK WHY ME, and I don't want to touch her because they always tell you that sort of thing, not to move someone who's fallen like this, but she's out cold and there's a phone there on the enormous desk, on top of which is also the package I've just delivered, and she evidently had time to open the package and all these vials of medicine are in there, have spilled out from inside the package, and I pick up the phone and call 911 and tell them there's a woman passed out and massively bleeding from her nose, and they ask who I am and what the fuck does it matter who I am, I'm thinking, can't they just get off their asses and send someone already, for all I know this Lydia Hall person is dead, and fuck, I hope I'm not somehow implicated in this, you hear about that kind of thing all the time, some poor fuck in the wrong place at the wrong time. Finally the Bensonhurst-sounding bitch at the other end of the phone says she's sending an ambulance and I just squat down and look at this beautiful woman on the floor bleeding on her carpet and I can't help but wonder, did she start bleeding like that because she didn't get the package of medicine in time. If Number Eleven hadn't wiped out then maybe both he and this Lydia Hall woman would be all right right now, and it's stuff like that that sometimes makes you feel like God is a senseless maniac.

The ambulance people get there pretty fast and get right to it with Lydia Hall, and no, she's not dead, they tell me, and they scoop her up onto a stretcher and put an oxygen mask on her face and cart her away just like that, leaving me in her apartment.

I stand there for about thirty seconds, frozen in my spot, not knowing quite what to do, then I go over to the desk where the package with the medicine is, and I start to look at the medicine vials, but the names of the drugs mean nothing to me even though my little sister Viva is a nurse and just loves being a nurse and whenever I see her is endlessly relaying all these medical anecdotes to me and pumps Lily, my daughter, full of this information. My sister has no kids of her own, is probably the lone girl from our projects that wasn't pregnant at fifteen, which, our mother loves to tell us, has to do with Pop being so educated, Pop being a disgraced engineering genius that got caught embezzling funds some twenty years ago, and so we went from our decent little apartment on the Upper West Side to living in the projects on Avenue D, at which point Pop pretty promptly just caved in and gave up and went over to India, where he'd spent a lot of his childhood—for Pop was half white, half Indian, Indian Indian, not American Indian, and supposedly Pop was going on some sort of spiritual quest and at first kept in touch with us but then basically disappeared off the face of the earth, leaving Mom so brokenhearted about it, just sort of giving up then, caving in for a while, letting herself go a bit but ultimately getting strong from it all and throwing all her energy at me and Viva, this working wonders with Viva, who really got her shit together, going to nursing school and whatnot, but me not faring so well, pulling some stunts with my boys what with the crack emporium on Eighth Street and me getting locked up a coupla times and then getting a few girls pregnant but only Delia going on to have a child, which I'm now glad for. I love my daughter, Lily. She's eight now and she's a really good-looking lively little kid and my sister Viva just totally dotes on her whenever I have Lily for the weekend. Viva is already steering my daughter in the direction of being like a quantum physicist or a neurosurgeon and so is endlessly making Lily memorize the names of diseases and things.

So I'm alone in this woman's apartment and I suppose I could just grab one of the vases or lamps that are all over the place, just stuff it in my messenger bag, and the price of it alone would probably support me a good six months off on some little island somewhere, never mind if I started hunting for jewelry or something, but I've put that kind of thing behind me. I was never proud of the stupid shit I pulled when I was younger, and yeah, I lived in the projects long enough to realize what kind of opportunity I have here in this woman's apartment, but she didn't seem like a bad woman, and anyway, if I took even the smallest thing, of course she would know it was me and I'd get fired from the messenger service and have to start from scratch yet again. So I just get out of there. I pull the door shut behind me and on the way out tell the doorman he might want to keep an eye on that apartment what with its mistress so suddenly out of commission, and the doorman nods at me coldly.

I go back out and get on the bike and of course it's still raining. I ride like hell to try and get all my shit plus Number Eleven's shit delivered and it's not till two days later, when Lydia Hall sends a massive flower arrangement to me at work, that I find out I probably saved her life by being there and calling 911. The enclosed note says she's immensely grateful and if there's ever anything I need, any way she can help, all I have to do is call. She's back at home now, and she's put her phone number on the card, and I just tuck the card in my pocket. I go into the back of the office to make a few phone calls, trying to reach my daughter, but she's not there, nor is my ex, and then, as I'm sitting there, feet propped up on the desk, Alfie comes in, just back from her runs. Her jeans are muddy and her freckled face, that looks so young to begin with, now looks more so, what with the smudge of dirt or bike grease over her nose and I get up and walk over to her and wipe the grime from her nose and steal a kiss, which surprises her, and she looks around nervously. We've kept our thing a secret here at work—lest the other messengers think our liaison means open season on Alfie, the lone female—and it's been two weeks since we slept together, not that I necessarily wanted it that way, just that she makes me feel awkward and I never know how to approach her, and she turns from me now, pulling out her sheath of receipts and setting it on the desk before stripping off her messenger gear. I watch with fascination as she takes off the skullcap into which she tucks her long blonde hair. I admire her transformation from boyish bike messenger into lovely young woman, the hair falling down over her shoulders, and now she peels off the extralarge sweatshirt and underneath she is wearing a tank top that sweetly hugs her small torso and diminutive breasts that require no bra.

"What are you looking at?" she says after a while, feeling my eyes on her.

"You."

"How come?" she frowns, but she is pleased.

"You're gorgeous," I tell her, and she rolls her eyes and turns her back to me.

"Bad day?" I ask her.

"Very," she says, turning back around, pulling up the leg of her jeans, and showing me a huge bruise over her shin.

"I got doored. I got rained on. Number Forty propositioned me."

"Oh," I say. "Look," I add brightly, not wanting the conversation to die. "I got flowers for saving some lady's life," I tell Alfie, pointing to the bouquet, which, it occurs to me, it might be nice to give to Alfie, but already in my head I've decided to go by my mom's and give it to her.

"Again?" Alfie says and I shrug because she's right, this is the second time in two weeks someone seems to think the fact of my delivering them a package has taken their fate on an upward swing, the previous time being when I had a package from I.C.M. to take to some guy's apartment over in Hell's Kitchen. The guy buzzes me up and I climb the five flights to his apartment and he rips the package out of my hands and starts reading the pages that are inside the thing before I've gotten a chance to have him sign for the package and he's holding these pages in his hands and he just starts to shake and his whole face knots up like a fist. "Hey," I say to him. "Hey, are you okay, guy?" And he's this very tall white guy, very pale, but now his face is turning funny colors and he's not saying anything, just shaking like that, reading whatever's on the pages and just panicking about it.

"Listen," I say to him, "I've got to get you to sign for this." I sort of wave the receipt at him but now he's losing it, he's thrown the pages down to the floor and is staring at a spot above my head with his lip quivering and he looks like he's really about to snap.

"Hey, look, what is it?" I say. "Is there something I can do?" And it's not like I'm some angelic being or anything, but this guy's really falling apart, and since he's not saying anything, just staring ahead like that, like a mental patient, I look down at the papers that have fanned out all over the floor, and after looking at them for a minute I see that they're rejection notes from publishers.

"So you're some kind of writer?" I ask the guy, and after a second he looks up at me and his face has gone totally blank.

"I'm some kind of writer, yes."

"What, you were trying to get a book published?"

"Yes," he says blankly. "I'm sorry. It's not your problem. Where do you need me to sign?"

At which I give him the receipt and he, with great effort, pulls himself together, taking the paper from me and holding it in his shaking hand, and I can see past him into the guts of his apartment and it looks dark and messy in there, like a guy in trouble lives in there, and all of a sudden I can't do this, I can't just leave this guy here, on his own, in this bad dark nest, and I say, "Look, you don't know me from a hole in the wall, but listen, I think maybe you should talk a little. I got a minute. Why don't you just tell me about it?"

And at first the guy's face just stays blank and nothing happens, and then some sort of light comes into his eyes. He looks

at me and then shrugs and stands aside, making a motion to in-
dicate I should come in. I end up sitting down in a stuffed chair
that smells of dust, and at first the guy says nothing but after a
while tells me his name, John, and then once he says that, it's
like the floodgates have opened and he just pours out all this
stuff about his personal heartbreak, how he quit drinking and
was living in the Salvation Army in Scranton, Pennsylvania, and
worked in an ammo factory and wrote a book, working into the
wee hours, hunkered down at the tiny desk in his room, and he's
been trying to hold it all together for so long, and now this is it,
he has put all of himself in this book. Now these letters his agent
has just sent him, these letters I've delivered to him—"Just look
at them," he says, picking them up, then letting them fan to the
floor again, like so many pieces of pain.

I say nothing to this. There is silence. Then John asks do I
want to go get a drink with him. I tell him I don't think that's a
great idea, wasn't he trying to not drink, and what would it do
to him if he drank on top of all this bad news. It just couldn't
be good.

He ended up agreeing with me but did come with me to get
sandwiches at a deli. We sat at one of those little tables in the
back, eating sandwiches, and then went our separate ways. He
crossed my mind later in the day and then, next thing I knew,
the guy had sent me this immense thing of flowers with a long
beautiful letter telling me how what I did, that bit of human
kindness I'd shown—and that's the term he used, *human kindness*—how that had saved him, and for all he knew, he'd have
been lying in a gutter now puking on himself or maybe dead,
and so Alfie was right in saying, "Again?" when I showed her
the flowers Lydia Hall had sent, because, yes, this had just happened about ten days earlier.

"Yeah." I smile down at Alfie. "Again. I know, it's stupid,
right?"

"What are you, Indio, guardian angel to the sad?" And I just look at her and I'm startled at what she's said, because I've sort of started to wonder this myself, and then I ask her can I come by her place a little later and she knits her eyebrows then shrugs and says, "Oh, yeah, sure, I guess," and I tell her not to get so overly enthused about the idea and she smiles and says, "Okay, Indio, yes, it'd be good if you came over," and I kiss her again and watch her walk down the hall, and her shoulders are overly muscled and big for her small physique, but it just adds ambiguity to her somehow and makes me want her all the more.

I ride down to my place that's just this jagged little apartment on Rivington Street, right off Bowery, where all sorts of neighborhoods border one another but it's really not a neighborhood of its own, and I go up to take a quick shower before going by Mom's, because what with having been a moderate fuckup, it's always best to be extra presentable, in particularly good form, when I go to see my mother nowadays.

I show up at Mom's and she's in her housedress but with her hair all tidy, her whole person so tidy like always and the most heartbreaking thing is that no matter which evening I choose to come by, Mom is always home. And although she keeps herself busy after work, maintaining a perfectly clean apartment amid all the chaos of these projects—as if she didn't put in enough time cleaning at the Marriott in the days, which is her job, head housekeeper—she is profoundly alone, so alone. She keeps apart from most of the crazy women that live here, she keeps apart from the other housekeepers at the Marriott, she is just apart, in her own little tidy world. I go in and present her with the flowers and she says, "Oh, Henry, you shouldn't have," and Mom is the only one ever allowed to call me by my given name, and I tell her that really, I didn't, some lady sent flowers thinking I'd had something to do with saving her life, and Mom pats my face with both her hands, looking up at me, and her eyes are wet, and then she turns quickly away from me lest tears roll down her tired cheeks.

Of course, she's got some rice and beans on the stove and immediately fries up some plantains too and then feeds me but good.

We don't talk about all that much. I mean, we never go into the depths of each other, but there is tremendous love between us, and now Mom urges me to stop over at Jojo's apartment, Jojo being one of Mom's lone friends, a hardworking guy from the neighborhood that Mom plays Scrabble with sometimes—my mom probably being the only person in these projects that plays Scrabble—and after Mom has fed me and told me that, yeah, work is still fine, after she has asked me, like always, isn't there a nice girl in my life, and me being vague about it, not thinking little blonde Alfie would be all that game to come meet my mother in the projects, I peck my mother on both cheeks and promise I'm going to go stop by Jojo's for a quick visit.

Jojo lives on Avenue D but not in the projects, rather in this old tenement building that now is mostly taken over by white kids and where Jojo has lived longer than most of them have been alive. He's way up on the top floor and when I knock it takes a while for him to come to the door. Not that long ago he had a stroke and the whole right side of his body isn't working so well. His mind is okay. But his body has a lot of lifeless areas that he has to sort of drag after him.

"Indio!" he says after he's looked through the little peephole then thrown open the door.

"Jojo, what's up?" I say and hug him. He's only about five six and weighs something like 120, just a rickety little guy. When he was younger he was an exercise rider out at Belmont, breezed racehorses in the morning, but it's dangerous work, you end up getting knocked around and stepped on and mangled with some frequency, and when Jojo got married in his late twenties, the missus didn't go in for that kind of thing and made him find a new job. Which is when he took over the Mister Softee truck from his uncle Pedro, which he ended up enjoying. The missus died of brain cancer some years back and they hadn't had any kids, and Jojo was grateful for the ice cream truck that kept him in contact with thousands of kids. In the winter sometimes he takes on odd jobs, helping neighborhood building superintendents with simple plumbing and construction. But what he loves is the ice cream truck. Now, though, since the stroke six months ago, Jojo hasn't been able to do much of anything. I think he gets disability, but it makes him unhappy. He prefers to work.

So I hugged Jojo and followed him inside that railroad apartment of his with all the faded 1960s flower-motif wallpaper designed for kitchens or children's rooms but that Jojo's late missus had put up in the whole place and that was now peeling off in great strips, like the skin of some sad psychedelic beast.

"You need a beer, Indio?" Jojo asks me, hobbling over to the fridge, and I tell him, "Sure," and we sit down at the skimpy kitchen table drinking our beers, and Jojo has the windows wide open although it's mid-February and he's going on about the balmy weather even though it's not exactly that warm out, and then he gets this light in his eyes. "Indio," he says, "I got an idea."

"What's that, Jojo?"

"Let's take the ice cream truck out. I went and got all the stuff ready last weekend when they were talking about a warm spell coming. You want? I can't do it by myself, Indio, but maybe you want to come along and drive? Say just a coupla hours? I'll split the take with you."

And his face is so full of a hope that pulls me in and I can't refuse him, so we go over to the parking lot Deno runs on Avenue C and get the ice cream truck out and we've already been in action a good hour what with the sinister distorted Mister Softee song piping out through the truck's crackly speakers and kids stumbling out of their buildings looking a little confused because February is not the time for the ice cream truck, but all the same they want ice cream, in fact everyone wants ice cream, not just the kids but also the white people, the old fat Dominican men who play dominoes, everybody, and then there's this little kid, Rutgers, lives just a few doors down from my mom and I've seen him around a lot. He's a strange-looking kid with blonde hair but dark skin and eyes. He's maybe the same age as my daughter, Lily, but anytime I see him, he's all alone, and Jojo and I have been on this particular corner of Seventh and D for some time and are ready to move on, but then Rutgers comes along. "Wha's up, Indio?" he says to me, cocking his head and kind of jutting out his jaw, not particularly trying to look tough but just going through the motions he sees all around him every day.

"Hey, Rutgers, what can I get you?" I ask him, for, right now, Jojo's taken a break. It's hard for him to stand up for a long time and he's in the driver's seat, taking a load off.

"I don't want any ice cream, Indio, I'm just hangin'."

"Yeah? So what's up? How are you?" I ask the kid like we're old pals, although I've probably only ever said ten words to him.

"I'm okay, I guess, but you know what I was thinking?" he says, cocking his head the other way now.

"What's that?"

"It's like this, Indio," he tells me, squinting his eyes up and planting his little fists on his hips, "I've been thinking about the world. I mean, what do you think, Indio, what do you think is the true story of the world?"

"What?" I ask him, not sure I heard right.

"The true story of the world. What is it?"

"Uh . . ." I'm totally stunned. The kid has really got me now. I mean, for one, I'm not sure exactly what he's asking me, but mostly it's his stance, the way he's holding himself, with all this thought radiating out of him, like some kind of little philosopher king or something.

"What do you mean exactly, Rutgers?" I ask him then, feeling like a dolt, like this little kid, who's the same age as my own daughter, definitely has insights I've missed.

"I mean everything, really everything. The true story of the world. How did the world happen, Indio? I don't think it was God that just said, 'Okay, here's a world,' and just made a world and people and dogs and trees, but then how did it happen? What was the first thing, Indio? What's the true story?" he asks me with his face so serious, and I'm not sure what gave him the idea to ask me this, and for all I know he goes around asking everyone, but it's certainly unexpected and incredibly charming and in a way gives me such hope. "Rutgers," I tell him, "people are endlessly arguing about that kind of thing. I mean, you got your big bang and you got your religions and maybe somewhere between the two is the true story."

"But where? Where is between the two?" Rutgers asks me now and he really looks disconcerted, like he's going to have trouble getting through his evening if he can't get the answer he needs. He's just this little kid, this little Puerto Rican kid in the projects, but he really needs the answer to the true story of the world, and I wish I could give it to him, I wish I could smooth things for him and take him out of whatever hideous family situation he's got going because I seem to remember he just lives with an aunt, which means probably his mother's a junkie or some such and his father could be one of any number of guys, and I want to tell the kid the true story of the world but have to admit I just don't know it. And long after he has shrugged one last time and accepted the free cup of vanilla I've offered him, after he's bopped off with that light yet lonesome child walk of his, long after Jojo has grown tired and we've brought the truck back round to Deno's parking lot and I've suddenly remembered how I had asked Alfie if I could come over and I've called her and told her how sorry I am and how I got distracted with Jojo and can I still come over, after all that, as I'm climbing the eight flights up to Alfie's place, it's haunting me, the true story of the world is haunting me, as are all the odd things that have piled up on me recently, like why are human beings so wretched to one another and animals don't do to one another what humans do to one another, they don't molest their children but just band together fighting off the predators, and there's a thing that's coming to life in me, there's a thing I'm feeling where I want to do that, I want to form a little clan of humans where we express kindness to one another, and sometimes I wish I'd made a go of it with Delia and we'd raised Lily like a family, but really it was Delia who didn't want any part of me and who can blame her, what with me looking like I was going the criminal route at the time and Delia had better offers and figured she'd find a good man to take care of her and our kid, and in fact she has, Delia's found herself an accountant and he's pasty and boring but he looks after his women and I'm carrying all these thoughts with me when I tap at Alfie's door.

She opens up and she's wearing a lovely Chinese robe, and her two dogs, immense white poodles that Alfie rescued when their circus careers were brought to an end by the onset of arthritis, the poodles start dancing in that odd way they have of doing, their hips stiff from the pain but none of this diminishing their fervor over greeting me. As I kiss Alfie hello and step through the threshold, I see that another woman is there, standing behind Alfie, a woman who looks startlingly like Alfie, only a bit older and wearing makeup and a skirt in a way Alfie never would.

"Indio, this is my sister, Katie," Alfie says, motioning to the woman.

I shake Katie's hand. "I'm sorry, I didn't know you had company," I tell Alfie, and I'm confused, for we did have plans.

"No, no, I'm just leaving," Katie says. "I was just retrieving my sweater," she tells me, holding forth a red sweater, and then she is out the door and Alfie and I walk down the skinny hall into the main room, where her bed and desk are, and the dogs are still dancing and I just put my arms around Alfie and hold her really tight, but her body feels frozen, like she wasn't expecting this outpour of warmth from me. Her guard is up and it is cold, so cold, and maybe it's my fault because I've never been terribly forthright with her, I've never expressed the many things she makes me feel, but I'm afraid and I know she is too and it makes me sad, for her, for me, for all of us, and I pull away from her, and lest I say something stupid, I ask for a glass of water.

"All I've got is tap," she says, getting a crease of worry in her forehead.

"It's okay, I'm not your bottled water kind of guy, Alfie," I say in a sort of chiding tone, because if there's one thing she ought to have learned about my character, this is surely it, but she's evidently feeling serious and doesn't smile or laugh at any of this, just fills up a glass and hands it to me and then goes to sit at the edge of her large bed and looks up at me with those unreadable green eyes of hers.

There are things human beings need to say to each other when they have been physically intimate but Alfie just freezes me up. She's from this more upscale background, not a rich kid, but lower middle class or something, and apart from her sister, Katie, she never mentions a family of any sort, whereas I'm always going on and on about my mom or my kid or my sister, and Alfie is in college and is incredibly smart, probably has one of those ridiculous IQs, for all I know is even a genius, but it makes her keep her mouth closed about everything, and in a sense she reminds me of the kid Rutgers, like Alfie probably has been trying to figure out the true story of the world all this time too and no one will tell it to her.

So I just start to talk because I'm nervous, and after I've blabbed on and on about my day and about Mom and Jojo with his stroke and his ice cream truck, I start to tell Alfie about Rutgers, how he came up to me, thinking I could somehow tell him the true story of the world.

"The true story of the world?" Alfie says and her mouth gets round and open with wonder, like this is the most beautiful thing she's ever heard.

"Isn't that amazing? Isn't it amazing that this little kid would ask me that?"

"Oh . . . ," Alfie says, and for a moment I think she's gonna start to cry, she seems so moved by it, and I go kneel at her feet with her still sitting on the edge of the bed and I wrap my arms around her calves and rest my head on her knees and she grabs my head, putting one hand on top, one under my chin, and we just cradle parts of each other like that for several long minutes. Eventually I get up on the bed next to her, nuzzle her neck, and start to tenderly undo her robe, with this feeling, this feeling I don't usually have.

We make love in a way that isn't quite ordinary and I see so much in her and I want to touch it but can't quite, and after a while, after we've made love and she's gotten up to put some classical music on the little CD player she's got, when she comes back to the bed and we share a cigarette and blow smoke rings in the air above our heads, all of a sudden I ask her how come she never has any condoms here, because I've started to wonder if maybe she just never has sex or if she's in the habit of having unsafe sex or what, and I know it's not the most poetic or romantic thing to be bringing up, but in my own way I guess I'm edging toward the monogamy thing because I know now that I'd like that with her, I'd like for her to be my girlfriend, I'd like to watch her be awkward around my daughter and my mother, it would be nice, but right away, as soon as I've asked, I see this wasn't such a great idea.

"Oh," she says, propping up on one elbow and looking directly at me, which she usually doesn't do.

"I'm sorry, was that a bad question?"

"No, it's okay. You should know."

"Know?"

"I'm a lesbian."

"You're what?"

"I like girls."

"But I'm a man," I say, which is ridiculous but is the first thing that comes out of my mouth.

"I know. Usually, though, I sleep with girls. So, no condoms."

"Oh."

"Is that okay?"

"Is what okay?"

"Well."

"I guess, sure, I just . . . I didn't know," I say, and what, how would I have known? Did it ever occur to her to tell me? Is that why it's been so hard to talk to her? The whole time she's thinking how I'm not a girl? Jesus. What the fuck. I guess this would put a damper on her being my girlfriend. So I don't say more about it. Right away I change the subject, asking about the music she's got on, and she tells me it's a guy named Stravinsky, and then Stravinsky leads to some other topics that have nothing to do with lesbianism, and although I'd planned on staying the whole night here with her, pretty soon I'm feeling caved in and I know I have to get home, and so, after a good interval, where I won't seem like a total creep for leaving even though I guess she mustn't care that much, I get dressed and kiss her lightly goodbye and I just go home to Rivington Street.

I make myself two pieces of raisin toast, not so much that I'm hungry as that I need to distract myself and what with the austere sort of life I've arranged here there's no TV and just the crappy old cassette player and nothing I really want to listen to and I munch toast and stare out the window where I can see into the Andrew Hotel there on Bowery, and it's an ancient place where nothing has changed in fifty years except for the inhabitants, scabby old guys with no teeth and wormy coats they wear year round and pants they've picked out of the garbage, the pockets of which probably don't often hold the six dollars it costs to sleep there, and I can see the guys faintly through the window. I can look into the TV room where their hunched forms assume positions of desperation, and it's not exactly a cheering sight, and finally I just lie down on the couch that also serves as my bed and I fall asleep because after all, it's been a long day.

It rains practically all week but I've brought the rain suit with me and it makes me think of Alfie, of course, and she even tells me how good I look in it, giving me this look with her big green eyes, and I don't know where to go with any of this and now I don't want to have sex with her anymore because I guess I'd gotten to hoping for something more, and it makes me feel like a girl a little, and all the roles in the world are played by the wrong people, and I just go about my business, in the rain, making a lot of runs because Number Eleven has had complications with infections in his face and Number Fourteen has been out on a crack run and Number Three is just plain stupid and there's a lot of work, and as I'm zipping all over this infernal city, I'm thinking how maybe I will call Lydia Hall, because you never know, right, I mean, she's a beautiful rich woman, what does she want with some bike messenger, but who's to say really, and then, one afternoon, just when I'm thinking how that day I'm going to call Lydia Hall, whose life she thinks I saved, I get this delivery over in Chelsea, to this high-rise on Eighth Avenue, and although there's a doorman, he's been told to send me up and bring the package right to the guy's door, and so I go up in the elevator and get off on the fifteenth floor and ring the bell on the door, but nothing happens except I hear these sort of ominous sounds coming from in there, like chairs getting turned over, and then I hear a guy's voice yelling and I keep ringing the bell anyway because I don't care what kind of chaos they've got going on, I've got to get on with my life such as it is, and then suddenly the door flies open and this guy looking completely insane screams "WHAT?" in my face and I say, "Messenger," and in the room behind him I see this woman with long black hair. She's opening the window and now getting up and standing there, on the ledge of this tall window, with nothing separating her from the wind and the fifteen-story drop, and my heart gets stuck in my throat, and meanwhile the guy is scowling at me furiously, with his back to the woman, and ripping the package from my hand, and I just wordlessly point at the woman in the window and the guy says "What?" at me and at last turns around and sees the woman in the window. "LUCY!!! NO!!!" he screams and races over to the woman.

"Don't come near me, Nathan, get away from me, this is enough, this is all too much, I'm going."

And, absurdly, I think of what a quaint way of putting it that is: "I'm going," like she's going to the store or something instead of plunging to her death.

"Lucy, no, Lucy, no, Lucy, no," the guy just wails and he's transfixed in this spot about a foot away from her and he's just not doing anything, so I walk over there, over to the woman.

"You get away from me," she says to me. "Don't move or I'll go," she says, and her face is this crazy thing, like an angry marble, what I guess is a pretty face but just all flushed up with chaos.

"It's okay, I'm not coming near you," I say, stopping right where the guy is standing, "but really, you should get down from the window."

"And do what?" she says to me.

"You just should get down. There's no reason to go."

"You're wrong," she says, but she's looking at me now, half turned around, like half of her is ready to stay here in the high-rise with this guy she's been fighting with.

"Maybe there are reasons to go, but there are reasons to stay too," I tell her.

She stares at me. Then her face bunches up and she starts crying. In a second her whole body is shaking with sobs and she's crumbling in on herself and the guy goes over to her and pulls her down from the ledge.

And I go then. Neither of them seems to notice. I don't bother with having them sign for the package or anything. I just go back down, past the doorman, and I get back on the bike and ride.

At least it's stopped raining.

ANIMALS

I woke up with that boiling sensation in my digestive tract again. The last thing I'd eaten was Chinese dumplings from the storefront place downstairs. I hadn't even been hungry but was harboring a crush on the surly Chinese lady that works in there. She hates me and, I'm sure, spits in my food or instructs her son to jerk off in White Devil's dumpling sauce. Which makes me like her even more. Only now I'd woken up with my gut doing backflips. Little shards of bean curd dancing down my intestines. Strange Chinese vegetables with names like prostitutes rumbling in my stomach.

I sat there for a long time. In my orange chair, with the stack of recyclable take-out containers in a pile next to it. Then I started to think of the dumplings those take-out tins had contained. And about the Chinese lady's son jerking off in them.

I went in the bathroom and threw up. Only bile, though. I guess the dumplings had long been digested. You never know with your body. Sometimes it has a way of secreting stuff away, and fourteen hours after eating dumplings, when it all should have long turned to effluvium, you end up vomiting a recognizable chunk of bean curd. Ever since I quit drinking, my digestion has been screwy. You'd think it'd be the other way around, but no.

I washed my face and brushed my teeth. Kitten came and rubbed against my leg as I stood looking in the mirror. I needed a shave. I ran a comb through my hair. It was getting long. And a little gray. I was looking creepy.

I turned to go back in the main room to try coming up with a game plan for the day. And then I saw it: another fucking rat, blatantly strolling across the floor, not even remotely nervous about my being there, just having a look around, like it was window-shopping in my kitchen.

The rats had first appeared a week earlier. A strange noise woke me in the middle of the night. I went in the kitchen and saw that Kitten was trying to get inside the big industrial-sized trash can. I came closer and heard this thumping noise from inside the can. I looked in, and a huge rat made a leap for my face. I swear to you. Like the thing was rabid or something. It made my blood run cold. I grabbed Kitten and backed away from the trash can as the rat kept on, making the horrible thunking sound, hurling himself against the side of the trash can. I stood frozen, holding Kitten, who was squirming, wanting to have a go at the rat that was twice the size of her. Finally I put the lid on the trash can and carried the whole thing downstairs and outside and just left it there, with the rat sealed inside for the garbage men to deal with.

The rat sought revenge, though. Two mornings later I stumbled into the main room to make coffee and there were six rats on the kitchen table, just hanging out there, like a pack of Dominican guys around a boombox, totally unfazed when I stomped my foot. I locked Kitten in the bathroom for safety and eventually, beating on the kitchen table with the broom, got the rats to vamoose. They all zipped under the sink. After a minute I got on all fours and peered down there, behind the cleaning products I never use, and sure enough, there was a rat-sized hole in the wall under my kitchen sink.

I hunted around for stuff to plug the hole and ended up taping two take-out tins over it with duct tape.

But now they were apparently back. When the rat finished inspecting my kitchen and at last went under the sink, I bent down to look, and wouldn't you know, the fucking beasts had chewed through the take-out tin. There were little rat teeth marks in there.

I started to panic. I mean, for one, rats carry all those diseases. Like bubonic plague, and by now, surely, some sort of mad rat disease, since spongiform encephalopathy craftily jumps species, from sheep to cows to humans, and certainly by now to rats. And these mad rats were doubtless itching to infect Kitten.

I locked Kitten in the bathroom while I went back to sit on the orange chair to try and think what to do.

I had sort of planned on going to A.A. that day. I'd started attending again. After my last girlfriend, Jody—who I really loved but who was totally out of her mind—nearly drove me back to drink trying to make me have sex with a hooker and then dumping me just because I wouldn't. I'd even bought a bottle of scotch but then ended up throwing it out the back window onto a Dumpster. The next day, I'd gone to an A.A. meeting and it wasn't all that bad. So I started going a few times a week, gravitating to down-and-out meetings with old bum guys or black crack kids who would be sober but still have an AK47 tucked in their pants for good measure. Luckily I hadn't run into this girl Laura, who'd initially turned me off

A.A. by fucking me and then never wanting to see me again and making big scenes whenever I turned up at meetings she attended.

That morning I'd planned on branching out and going to a more upscale meeting over in the West Village. Only now I was afraid the rats would eat Kitten. So I put her in my gym bag and took her with me.

I got there a little late and all the seats were taken. I had to stand in the back, peering over some guy's shoulder to try and see the girl who was telling her life story—which happened to be a good story. The girl was youngish. From France. Had that whole French thing going, that sort of steamy propriety or what have you, with smooth dark hair and not bad looking, only her teeth were too big for her face. She told about leaving France and being a go-go dancer in New Jersey and hanging out with these motorcycle thugs. One day she was riding on the back of some guy's Ducati. She had hot pants on and was so drunk she had her leg against the burning hot engine, only didn't even feel it. When she pulled her leg away, she left half her leg flesh stuck to the Ducati engine. The motorcycle guy told her to just go put ointment on her leg. A few days went by and her leg was turning green. One afternoon, she was stand-ing in the lobby of some hotel to meet some guy. She had a miniskirt on in spite of her leg. This young veterinary student happened to walk by and saw her leg and told her she was about to lose that leg and she should come with him. He ended up taking her to the hospital, where they told her she was a few hours away from amputation, but they saved her leg and the guy had her move in with him and eventually marry him. Then she started breaking into his samples of animal tranquilizers, shooting up all these things with names like ROMPUM and going into blackouts, and finally the husband kicked her out. Now she couldn't even go-go dance anymore since her leg was so scarred up.

Her face got cloudy when she told about her low point. Her "bottom," as they call it.

She ended up doing phone sex and drinking herself blind and insulting all the heavy breathers until one of her phone sex coworkers turned out to be in A.A. and dragged her to a meeting. That's the fairy-tale part. She stopped drinking and eventually the husband took her back, and she started popping out kids and being happy.

So I'm still stuck there in the back of the A.A. meeting and by now Kitten's upset at being in the gym bag so I take her out of there. Just then, this guy with no teeth that drinks turpentine and routinely turns up at meetings to stand in the back stinking and shouting at the women that they're whores, he shows up and stands at my back. By now I've got Kitten propped on my shoulder and of course the toothless guy takes note: *"Pussy, pussy, pussy,"* the guy starts saying to my cat. Which is totally offending me, never mind the twenty-some-odd upstanding sober women in the A.A. meeting. So then this big gay guy wearing leather gets up and escorts the toothless guy out and then shoots me this filthy look and says, "No pets in the meeting."

So I go stand outside, dejected, Kitten still on my shoulder, and then, don't you know, fucking Laura materializes.

I mean, you see her coming from fifty blocks away, that walk she has, tits first, and the sway of her wide hips and I'm just thinking, FUCK, right, and I take Kitten off my shoulder to put her back in the gym bag so we can get the hell out of there before Laura causes a scene, but already Laura's upon us and you just never know with women, because she's all smiles now, and last time I saw her she was like Linda Blair with her head spitting insults at me, and now she's smiling and walks up to me too close.

"Jack," she purrs, "is that your kitty cat?" And she tilts her head at me and bats her eyes and she's put on some weight but she's the kind of girl where it doesn't really matter, most of it just goes to her tits, and really the only danger is they'll get so big she'll topple forward, but it's not like she's ever going to have trouble getting laid, what with her whole sexy shtick and the sort of understated but elegant way she dresses, but always, as if by accident, with a bra strap showing here or a nice little pocket of flesh there.

So she's nice to me and it turns out she's the one who dragged that French girl to her first A.A. meeting and now is the French girl's sponsor, which means Laura's the one dispensing advice, and I can't imagine what kind of advice Laura would have to lay upon someone, but anyway, Laura then says it's her birthday today and I say, "Oh, well, hey, well happy birthday, Laura." Then, of all things, she invites me to a birthday party she's having that night at a restaurant in the East Village. "Please, Jack," she says, resting one hand on my arm and petting Kitten with the other, "please come, Jack."

So I don't know what to make of it. Like what kind of sick-bitch tricks does she have up her sleeve now. Maybe it's a trap. I don't know, but I guess I'm curious and besides, I like to put myself in these odd and extreme situations, so I say, "Yeah, sure, I'll come."

And she smiles and wiggles at me before going inside the A.A. meeting.

I put Kitten back in the gym bag and start walking away from there before something else weird happens.

And not like I know what to get that psycho girl as a present and I guess I'm supposed to get her one, but what do you get when you're an unemployed guy buying a gift for a girl you fucked once and who subsequently went snake on you?

So I get her this little candle from one of the Santeria places on Essex Street, not far from where I live. I go in there sometimes and I don't know the first thing about Santeria, I'm just a white guy, I can't even speak Spanish, but I always go in the place because somehow I like the suspicious look the woman in there gives me. And she's hot too in that sort of fat-Puerto-Rican-lady-in-man-made-fabrics way, and I love those ladies. I always wanted to get one to have sex with me but they never will. And certainly not this here Santeria witch with lipliner six shades darker than her lipstick making her mouth look like a rectum.

So I'm inspecting all the mysterious powders and incenses and statues and crazy candles with strange inscriptions to saints and I figure chances are this woman's got a coupla chickens in the back waiting to have their heads hacked off in sacrifice or whatever they do with those chickens. Puerto Rican people on the Lower East Side have a lot of chickens, less now than in the early eighties but still some, and then it occurs to me maybe there's a Santeria thing for the rats, right, like maybe they've got some weird rat poison Santeria powder or something, I don't know, so I say, " 'Scuse me, *signora, per favor, poison poro los ratas,*" and she gives me the nastiest look, right, doesn't say anything, just looks at me like I'm the lowest form of cockroach, and after a while, still looking at me but not moving at all, she opens her mouth and screams "MANUEL" at the top of her lungs, bloody screaming like I'm trying to ram statues of baby Jesus up her ass, and then an old guy appears and he's wearing a robe and this kindly expression until he sees I'm a white guy and then he just frowns.

"What you want?" he asks me.

"I wonder if you know how I can get rid of the rats. I have

rats infesting my apartment. Can you help me? Is there a powder or something? Do you have any insight?" I ask him, and I actually say *insight* to the guy, just in case he understands me, so he doesn't think I'm condescending to him as some loopy old Puerto Rican Santeria fuck. And the guy keeps looking at me, then stares down at the lady, and I don't know if she's his daughter or his wife or what, and I'm pretty sure they're going to put a terrible curse on me or take me out back to dance with the chickens, I don't know. Then finally the guy says, in perfect American English: "Try Brillo pads."

"Huh?" I say.

"Brillo pads," he says. "Rats hate Brillo pads. You get yourself a bit of plaster and mix it in with Brillo pads and plug up the hole they're coming through.

"You know where they're coming through, right?" he says then, all the sudden thinking maybe I'm such a moron I don't even have that much figured out.

"Yeah, yeah, of course, I know the hole," I tell him and he nods his head.

"Yeah, well, that's it, Brillo pads. They won't chew through that," he assures me.

"Hey, wow, thanks," I say, and I purchase a nice little candle for Laura, a red one with some sort of crazy invocation written on the side. As I walk to the door, I feel the raccoon Santeria lady's eyes burning into my back so I turn around and beam a huge smile at her. But she just frowns.

On the way home I stop off at the bodega on the corner of East Broadway and Essex to buy some Brillo pads—which they have even though it's a crack bodega. Two things crack bodegas always have are kitty litter and Brillo pads, and for good measure I buy Kitten some kitty litter too and the guys in the bodega look at me with their faces tight and their hands close to their pockets, where presumably they've got rocket launchers or sawed-off shotguns in the event I'm a narc or an enemy of unspecified nature. I stop off at the Chinese hardware store for plaster and the little guy in there is all smiles and I'm not sure if he thinks I'm an idiot and is laughing at me or if he's just friendly, but I grin right back at him, as if buying plaster is the highlight of my life, and then I go home, lock Kitten in the bathroom, and get busy stirring up the mixture to plug up the rat hole.

After some time I've got it ready and I apply it, half expecting an angry rat to poke his head through the still-drying concoction. At one point I do hear a sort of throttled shriek and I back away from the hole, but no rats appear, and finally I apply the last of the goop and sit back to admire my handiwork. I'm pleased with myself and I let Kitten out of the bathroom, then sit in the orange chair and look at the candle I've bought for crazy Laura. I have a moment of peace, what with having accomplished quite a bit in the day. I rest my head on the back of the chair and sit there vaguely wondering what the inscription on the side of the candle says and also debating whether or not I should try eating again, like how my digestive tract would welcome this and what exactly I could put in there that wouldn't upset it. I'm just sitting there, relaxed and nearly falling asleep, when all the sudden I realize it's already afternoon and I've got to go out to Brooklyn to walk my horse.

Although I'm just a guy with rats and borderline cirrhosis of the liver, I actually have a horse. One day I saw an ad in a New Jersey newspaper. A whole page of animals for adoption. Not cats and dogs, though. Barnyard animals. Like a lot of goats, some pigs, and, get this, two horses. The ad has pictures of the animals and little descriptions of their plights and I see this pretty brown horse with a long white blaze down her nose. The brief biographical note tells me the horse is nine and her name is Rosa. She was rescued from racing people who abused her and she needs a good home and right away I feel it: an overwhelming need to adopt this horse.

It's not like I come from some outdoorsy background. I grew up in Jersey City. My parents were welfare alcoholics until later in life, when they became born-again Christians and got a little storefront electrolysis business. So I'm hardly your horse-oriented sort of person. But looking at the picture of Rosa the horse, I just get seized and I end up calling about her. The lady on the phone tries to put me off when I admit I don't really know about horses but I'm determined, and the next day I go out there, to Summit, New Jersey, to this farm on the outskirts of town, and I visit the horse Rosa and I just love this horse. She has a gentle expression and they put a lead rope on her and I walk her around and she just goes along with it, and on the spot I say I want to adopt her.

They try to put me off again, saying Rosa needs to go to someone who can train her and keep her busy and happy, and although I obviously don't know how to train her, I could try to learn and could certainly make sure she's happy.

They just wouldn't go for it, though. Tried to get me to adopt a duck. But I didn't want a duck. I persisted trying for Rosa. I found a barn out near the park in Brooklyn where they'd let me keep Rosa for three hundred a month—which of course I didn't have, but now I work that much harder at my criminal activities, run a few extra short cons on tourists in Chinatown, and manage to come up with the money for Rosa's board. I went back out to Jersey, told the people how I'd found a nice stable and was going to take extremely good care of the horse, and they finally succumbed. I adopted Rosa and had her shipped to Brooklyn.

Of course, right away, it threw a wrench in my lifestyle: where before I'd only had to bring in $34.60 a day to keep afloat on rent, food for me and Kitten, and utility bills, now I had to tag on an extra ten dollars a day for Rosa's upkeep. This not even counting the farrier and occasional vet visits. So, within a week of adopting Rosa, I had new stresses in my life, what with worrying that bad weather would keep the tourists away or maybe someone would try to blow up the World Trade Center again or fucking Godzilla would strike and keep the Germans and the suckers from Ohio at home. I started taking bigger risks shoplifting. Used to be I'd just boost drugstore products, food, small pieces of clothing. Now, though, I risked felony charges, stealing snazzy menswear. I even had the balls to hit Barneys, which actually wasn't that remarkable since, the way I look, it's hard to tell if I'm some deliberately disheveled successful artfuck or just a down-and-out guy, and to be safe, those gleaming homo sales guys assume the former and they don't even have security tags on the fucking clothes at that place, but I bet they'll start soon, what with the likes of me depleting their wares to the tune of several thousand dollars in one week—after which I allowed myself a little vacation and spent many hours a day out at the barn with my horse, learning the ropes of horse care from this Puerto Rican kid Eddie that works out there. Eddie's a remarkable kid, has all these tattoos and whatnot that would look stupid on some white boy from the suburbs but look all right on this Spanish kid who earns a living mucking horseshit and rides a wild-looking paint pony.

Now, a few months into equine ownership, I've got it all worked out so I scam tourists in the morning, go out to the stable and walk Rosa around the park in the afternoon, and then shoplift in the evening, either before or after A.A. About once a week the kid Eddie gives me some sort of lesson. Not riding, 'cause I don't want to bother my horse by monkeying around on her back, but doing what they call free schooling, where you teach your horse to listen to your voice commands and whatnot. Eddie's shown me all the fine points of grooming and what to look out for, like the thrush they get in their hooves. He's also helped me train Rosa so she walks with me calmly through the traffic circle outside the barn and safely into the park. Everyone thinks I'm insane because I just have this pet horse that I walk like she's a dog, but what do I care. I love my horse.

Now I check on the status of the Brillo-and-plaster mix but I don't trust that it's quite dry so I take Kitten with me in the gym bag, figuring she'll enjoy herself out at the barn. I catch the F train out and it's a nice day, winter still but sunny, and Eddie's not around today, only Desmond, this Jamaican guy who mucks out the stalls and also has a horse but fell off his bike and slipped a disk and can't ride right now.

I put Kitten inside the tack room to let her play with all the brushes and tack and whatnot because I don't want her darting under the horse's feet. I say hello to Desmond, who says, "Mon, my back, mon, it is killing me, Jack, it is bad, I cannot do this anymore."

Desmond shakes his big head full of long skinny dreadlocks. He's got the pitchfork in one hand and the other hand pressed into the middle of his back, and he's wearing elaborate layers of filthy old cotton clothes, and I'm sure he's right, he shouldn't be mucking out stalls and carrying heavy buckets of water, and I end up helping him for a while and he's going on about how he's going to have to send his horse upstate to live in a field and he himself will have to retire for a while from his stable job, get a security job at the Brooklyn Museum like he used to have until his back heals, and I just nod my head and muck out two stalls, and after a while, I go to do my thing with Rosa.

When she sees me coming, Rosa's ears point forward. I go in, put my arms around her neck, and breathe in the comforting smell of her. After a minute she gets impatient, so I start brushing her off, going over her back and legs and pulling pieces of straw from her tail. Eventually I put the halter on and take her out to the park, where, of course, people give me crazy looks and try to talk to me about my horse, but I've cultivated this don't-fuck-with-me look for these occasions, coming off like a complete crazyman, so no one usually bothers me. Today, though, this girl on Rollerblades, a sort of yuppie law-school-looking blonde, approaches me. She's wearing one of those ridiculous getups involving tight shiny things and knee pads, and although, naturally, the mind drifts to the long hours a girl with knee pads could spend on her knees, blowing you till she'd sucked the last gasp from you, she's just not my type at all. Yet for some reason these yuppie-looking girls always like me, citing my kind of thug look as sexy because I guess I have this stuff in my eyes, in my facial expression, that makes them think I'd call them whores and fake rape them like they invariably want and my face is really a misnomer, because actually, I'm fairly straight sexually and like to just fuck a lot but not necessarily with mind games involved. Nonetheless, I endlessly attract these total psycho nympho girls and so the blonde pulls over on her godawful Rollerblades and says, "Hey, is that one of the horses from Windsor Stables?" and I say, "Well, yeah, I keep her there, yeah," and the girl goes, "Oh, she's *your* horse?" like I'm thug enough to fuck her but too thug to own a horse, and I say, "Yes, she's my horse," and the girl looks like she's about to pop a gasket over the concept of a thug with a horse and I say, " 'Scuse me, I gotta go," and I immediately turn Rosa in the opposite direction, leaving the yuppie to presumably jerk herself off so hard it scabs over.

By 4 P.M. I had put Rosa away, retrieved Kitten from the tack room, and caught the subway back to Manhattan.

I got home and still couldn't think of what to eat that wouldn't upset my stomach, so I just didn't.

I fed Kitten, then wrapped the Santeria candle for Laura in some Chinese newspaper, and although the plaster-and-Brillo concoction was dry by now, I had residual paranoia about the rats eating Kitten and so brought her with me to attend crazy Laura's birthday dinner.

I arrived a little late and there were about fifteen people, mostly girls, crowded around a table at one end of the restaurant. I got tense the moment I walked in, thinking I'd really made a mistake in coming here, all these girls throwing back their heads and laughing and a couple of men but all of them looking incredibly gay and well dressed.

"Oh, Jack, hi," Laura says, seeing me. "Come here, sit," she says, patting a spot next to her on the booth's seat and making a cute girl move over so there's space for me between Laura and the cute girl, and Laura's sudden enthusiasm for me is very strange: I don't know how the fuck I went from undesirable creep to the guy Laura wants sitting next to her at her birthday dinner, but all I can think is she just wants a lot of people who admire her to gather for the occasion. I'm not sure why she'd think I'd admire her after her psycho behavior, but, of course, on some level I do. I sit down and Kitten is contorting in her bag so I immediately have to pop her out of there—to the shock of all the gay guys and the delight of the cute girl sitting on my left.

"Oh, a kitty!" the cute girl says. "You take her everywhere?"

"No, not usually," I tell the cute girl, "but see, I had this, uh . . . rat problem and was afraid they'd eat her, so, uh . . ."

I stop then because I see one of the gay guys looking at me with revulsion and Laura, I can tell, is already wondering why the fuck she invited me, but the cute girl is beaming over all this and has her hand in my lap, scratching under Kitten's chin, and then tells me she's got three cats of her own and I see that she has the most amazing eyes, green eyes, and although three cats seems excessive, having a pet horse probably does too.

"I'm Katie, by the way," the girl adds, and I tell her I'm Jack and this prompts Laura's introducing me to all the other people at the table and then confiding that her and Katie met when they both used to work at the phone sex place and Katie's the only one at the table who's actually not in A.A.—which makes me warm to her all the more.

"But my father was an alcoholic lion tamer," Katie tells me then, "and I always end up with alcoholics for friends or even lovers, so I'm practically an honorary member of A.A. by now," she says with a smile on her small curved mouth.

"What? Your father was a what?" I ask her.

"Alcoholic." She shrugs.

"No," I say, "I mean, lion tamer, is that what you said? Your father was a lion tamer?"

"Oh, right, yes," she says, "a lion tamer. He's dead, though."

"I'm sorry," I say then as a bunch of food arrives.

The restaurant has some kind of Swiss motif going. The waitresses wear lederhosen with snowflake-patterned suspenders and the whole place stinks of strong cheese.

I haven't put in an order, having gotten there late and being worried about the joint being too pricey for me, and I'm not particularly hungry anyway. I just figure I'll sit here, not eating, and later, on the way home, I'll pick up some papaya or something that will agree with my stomach. The lederhosen waitress sits the platters of food down and it seems they've ordered several doses of fondue for the table, and pretty soon Laura is stabbing croutons and dipping them in cheese and trying to feed them to me and I'm still not sure what she wants from me, if she wants an encore presentation of our one-night stand or what, but she's leaning in very close to me, cooing at me to *open wide,* and between the stink of the cheese and the proximity of crazy Laura's enormous chest, it's a bit much. Yet it's easier to accept being fed like this than to say no, and I end up letting her feed me many pieces of cheese-covered bread and before I know it, it's all threatening to come back up and pour forth onto the festively laid dinner table and I suddenly plop Kitten into Katie's lap and excuse myself and, holding back the nausea, stumble into the bathroom, where I partly miss the toilet bowl and spew a bit on the floor.

When I get back to the table, I firmly refuse to be fed anymore and I try soothing myself with thoughts involving Katie, who sits there, right next to me, with Kitten still in her lap, as she takes lots of small bites of fondue.

Katie looks a lot like that actress Lili Taylor—only with dirty-blonde hair and freckles. Everyone I know wants to fuck Lili Taylor. She's just one of those people, not conventionally beautiful but so sexy and genuine seeming, and almost every guy I've ever talked to, white, black, Spanish, Chinese even, they all want to fuck Lili Taylor. And I know women who don't usually have dyke inclinations but you mention Lili Taylor and their eyes milk over and you're pretty sure they're going to have to race to the bathroom and jerk off for a while. So Katie looks a fair amount like Lili Taylor, with those sort of sweet determined features and these great big green eyes, and I figure everyone in the world must want to fuck her and the thing is, I don't. I mean, I don't immediately want to crawl under the table and go down on her or walk over and stick my dick in her mouth or things, I want to protect her. She looks so vulnerable, with this face that's wide open and full of brightness, she's really the most beautiful girl I've ever seen in my life and I want to make sure nothing bad happens to her—although the fact of my being attracted to her pretty much guarantees a lot of bad things have already happened to her because that's how I am, attracted to wounds and damage and the potential for healing these.

And then Katie's leaning over toward crazy Laura and starts telling a story about a guy she fucked, how his dick was so huge it was uncomfortable and one time the guy tried to fuck her in the ass with it and she turned to him and grabbed his big dick in her fist and said, "You're not putting THAT in my ass." And the gay guys almost lose it over that one and Katie's kind of got a foul mouth, which reassures me because immediately that eliminates eighty percent of the guys who would fall in love with her, because although guys like to fuck foulmouthed girls, they don't really want to take them home to Mom, where the girl might start spouting off like she's got sexual Tourette's or something, talking about dicks at the dinner table.

Somehow, and I don't know how, I made it through that meal, and then the fates were on my side because Katie asked which way I was walking and I'd heard her mention living in Hell's Kitchen, so I motioned toward uptown although, of course, I live downtown, and Laura said she was heading west in a cab, didn't Katie want a lift, and Katie shook her head no, and Laura looked at us both and suddenly her face got cloudy like it did the times she went off on me, and so I was fearing the worst because, although Laura wasn't going to make a move on me that night, I guess she didn't want to watch me skip off with some other girl, and just when Laura looked like she was about to say something, one of the gay guys, I think his name was Ricardo although he was Aryan looking, Ricardo grabbed Laura's elbow and said, "Honey, I'm taking you home," and made this suggestive face—although, of course, we all knew he'd rather have his fingers amputated than reach them under Laura's skirt, and Katie and I absconded together into the thick night.

"Isn't it just like Fritz Lang?" Katie asked me at one point.

By then we were walking across Twenty-fifth Street off Third Avenue and a lot of the buildings had scaffolding over them, reminding me of Rome, of the way all the beautiful ancient things there are endlessly being cleaned up and brightened, sometimes to the detriment of the things that looked better bearing the scars of centuries, and I told Katie that, actually, it reminded me of Rome but, yes, of *Metropolis* as well. Katie smiled. "Rome, yes," she said, exalted, and I could see she loved Rome as I do, and for a moment we grew quiet over this as it's no small thing, and at one point I took her elbow to guide her away from a pile of dog crap she was about to step in.

"But where do you live, Jack?" she asked me then, letting me keep my hand on her elbow a fraction longer than was necessary, and she was so beautiful, like an elf, a sprite, a spirit, a diva, and finally I confessed that really I live way downtown, not at all in this direction.

"But look," I told her, gesturing at the night, "it's so creamy out, the night's like soup, and I mean that in a good way. Let me just walk you wherever you're going."

"Don't you have a job to get up and go to in the morning or anything?" she asked then, arching her little eyebrows at me.

I shrugged. "Don't worry," I said, because of course I wasn't going to confide being a petty thief, not right then anyway, and I just said, "Don't worry," again, and then she shrugged and we kept on, walking and discoursing on things, books and streets and cities and cats, and I had taken Kitten out of the bag again and she was perched on Katie's shoulder now and the few people we passed on those streets looked and then quickly looked away, figuring someone with a cat on their shoulder was just as bad as any crazyperson you'd find anywhere.

After a while, we were on Katie's block, on Fortieth Street.

"I'm sorry," she said, looking up at me through thick lashes, "I know you've walked me all the way up here and maybe you need a drink of water or something, but my place is a mess and you really can't come up. I just don't want you to see it like that."

We were standing in front of a dank little Chinese restaurant and for a second I thought of how we both live above Chinese restaurants and I had hope about the way Katie said she didn't want me to see her place *right now,* implying there would be a time when I could see her place and I shrugged and said, "Okay. It's okay."

"If you want I can run up and get you a glass of water, though. Do you need a glass of water?" She pulled her little eyebrows together and her forehead accordioned with concern and I thought of what an odd thing it was to offer and maybe it was because surely I smelled of vomited fondue but I just told her, "No, I'm okay. Really, I'm okay."

And then she got up on her tiptoes and kissed me, her lips lingering on mine slightly, and all I could think was how strongly I must have smelled of cheese and I hoped she wouldn't hold this against me.

And then she was gone, swallowed into the darkness of her building's hallway.

I walked to Sixth Avenue to get the subway and I sat there, in the cold empty station, Kitten on my lap. We both watched rats eating detritus off the electric third rail.

The next day, although the Santeria Brillo/plaster concoction seemed to be keeping the rats out, I nonetheless brought Kitten with me in my travels. She rode on my shoulder and it actually helped when I was shoplifting or running short cons on tourists. Although a guy with a cat on his shoulder was doubtless a weirdo, no such guy could do anything criminal. The people I conned that morning had really fallen for Kitten. In fact, it if weren't for her, I don't think it'd have worked. They were this couple from some suburb. Both of them in khaki shorts and bouncy white sneakers and the guy with a beer gut stretching his Chicago Bulls T-shirt and his eyes beady and sunken in the flesh of his face. I'd seen them gawking at the baubles in a store on Mott Street and I sidled up to the guy, telling him how I could show him how to take the wife up to an authentic Chinese opium den and of course the guy demurred. "We're not those kind of people," he said.

"Of course you're not. Neither am I, but the first time someone took me up there, I can't tell you how rich an experience it was, *a genuine New York experience,*" I told him. "You just give me ten dollars and I go and bribe the little guy they got at the door up there, and then I come down and get you two," I said, but the guy wasn't going for it and I was just about to give up when the wife came over to scratch at Kitten's neck and coo over what a cute little cat she was and that was pretty much it. In a few more minutes I had their lousy ten bucks and I went up into the building, one I use a lot, a sweatshop actually, where I climbed up, as usual, all the way to the roof, then crossed three roofs over to emerge on Grand Street ten bucks richer and very pleased with Kitten.

The only place I didn't bring Kitten was up to John Jay College, to my classes, because it's a very serious atmosphere up there, what with almost all the students over thirty and really obsessive about studying because their time on earth is running out and they want to get on with it, get a career—which isn't at all my motivation. I can't ever imagine myself with a career, but if I keep at it much longer, I will have a master's in criminal psychology, which I doubt I'll ever use, but you never know.

• • •

Five days after meeting Katie, I'm sitting at home in the orange chair and Kitten's licking the rind from the papaya I just ate, and finally I call Katie. With trepidation. Almost wanting never to call her because I don't know how to act with her even though it was so easy to walk with her that night.

Right away she says to come over. Just like that. Right then. Even though it's the middle of the morning. She says to bring Kitten too, and now, as I walk into Katie's apartment, her cats all come sniffing at Kitten, who hisses and, when I put her down, runs with her belly to the ground until she finds a couch to hide under. I'm a little worried about my cat but then forget about it because Katie has made us lunch, she says—although certainly I can tell just by the burning smell in her apartment—and I look around a little. It's a big messy loft-type thing with a bed shoved over in one corner and huge blurry photographs of body parts stuck to the walls with pushpins.

Katie's actually got an apron on and I follow her into the kitchen, where she negotiates with these awful blackened mushrooms and some sort of grain she's cooked up. She puts it in two bowls, then we carry it back into the main room and sit on the couch.

I force some of the food down in spite of feeling certain it'll make me throw up. Katie's eating in lots of frantic little bites. Much as a cat would. Not putting a whole lot in her mouth each time but really attacking the whole process with gusto.

"You don't like mushrooms," she says all the sudden, scowling at me.

"I'm fine with mushrooms. I just have digestive problems. Recurring digestive distress."

"Oh?"

"Yeah."

And then, because I don't want to explain about it or gross her out with minute details of my intestinal distress, I put my bowl down and lean over and kiss her. She puts her own bowl down and starts sucking my mouth into hers, kind of chewing on my lips. We're side by side on her couch and now she straddles me and then I just lose it. Any control I'd meant to have just flies out the window and part of it is the apron. I've never in my life been with a woman who would wear an apron ever, never mind on a first date like this, and it just makes me want to rip into her, to fuck her hard. So hard.

I peel off pieces of her clothing. She has black cotton panties on and no bra. Her tits are like little saucers, pale with light pink nipples. I bite one and slide my finger in one side of her panties and watch her squirm. I bend her back, arching her over my arm; then, pulling her panties to the side some more, I go inside her. I go in and out, faster and faster, and she's making gasping sounds and sometimes these little yowls and her long pale hair is getting nests and sweat in it.

I stick my dick in her everywhere. Her ass, her mouth, her armpit. She sucks me, licks me, rubs me with her ass and her tits and her face.

Finally she pulls me in her so deep I wonder if I'll ever find my way out. We lock eyes in a way that would ordinarily make me throw up, but there's nothing sentimental in her eyes, just a firm soul, radiating the colors of strange lakes as I slide in and out of her, as I flip her onto her stomach, as I pull her onto the floor, as I drag her in the bathroom and turn the shower on and fuck her in there and then on top of the toilet bowl, me sitting on it, her sitting on top with her back to me, and then I make her put the apron back on and get on all fours on the floor and I fuck her there, and then take her out into the hallway and shove her against the banister and fuck her with a cold draft shooting up the stairs, and then someone is coming in the building and we both laugh and rush back inside her apartment, but we're pretty sure whoever it was must have seen our naked asses, and then we go stand right in front of the enormous picture window facing the Port Authority and we fuck. If people stepping off buses happen to look out through one of the tiny porthole windows on that side of the Port Authority, they'll get quite a view, like a big welcome to New York.

"Listen," I say to Katie after I've rescued Kitten from the broom closet Katie's cats have backed her into, "I have to go walk my horse. I have this horse, see. In Brooklyn. And I gotta go walk her."

Katie just looks at me and doesn't say a word. She's lying on the floor, naked, with her hair all matted. She keeps her eyes on me and reaches up for a cigarette on the coffee table.

"What are you talking about, Jack? Are you crazy?" she says finally.

And I know she doesn't just mean crazy as in the way normal people get crazy. She's asking if I have a history of institutionalization.

"No. None of that. Not crazy. But I do have this horse. Her name is Rosa. Why don't you come with me?"

Katie's smoking now. Same way she eats, intensely, with gusto.

Eventually, I start dressing her. She still hasn't said anything other than to ask if I'm crazy. But she lets me dress her. Then I go in the bathroom and find her hairbrush and start brushing the nests out of her hair. Finally she utters an "Ow" as I tug the brush through her mane.

We don't say that much on the train ride out. I've got Kitten back in the gym bag and now and then I say something to Katie. I ask her about her lion tamer father but she doesn't want to talk about that right now. I ask her what she does for a living. Is she a photographer? Are those photos in her apartment, those huge photos of body parts, are those part of her repertoire? She says yes on the photos but no, she's not a professional photographer. She doesn't volunteer what she actually does do for money. I know she used to do phone sex. With crazy Laura. So I start to wonder if she's a go-go dancer now.

"Are you a go-go dancer?"

"I'm too old for that, Jack, and they all have silicone anyway," she says, grabbing her own small tits, to the horror of a nice old Brooklyn lady across from us.

"I work for a forensic psychologist," she says after a pause, "sometimes even in the morgue. I look at dead bodies with him."

"What, he does autopsies of their psyches?"

"Sort of. Mostly he testifies in court. But sometimes he looks at bodies to see about traces of whatever led to the death."

"Oh," I said.

I wanted to ask her exactly what she did for the guy but I never did. I still haven't.

It wasn't until after we'd gotten to the barn, gotten Rosa out, and were walking into the park that I guess Katie finally believed me about the horse. Then she asked what the hell I was doing with a horse. Didn't I ever ride my horse. I explained the whole thing and Katie looked at me, at first with suspicion, then starting to laugh. Crinkling up her eyes.

"You just have a pet horse?"

"Yeah," I said, a little defensive. I thought she would understand.

"Don't get mad," she said then, reaching over and touching my face. "It's the best thing I've ever heard. I've gone out with all kinds of guys. Even guys with horses. But no one just had a horse. Just for horse company. I love horses."

So then she ends up telling me about her lion tamer father and how she grew up in the circus. On the road. And of course there were horses and she knows a great deal about them, including their history.

"Do you know," she says, "in the mid–nineteenth century, in Hell's Kitchen, before they had the elevated trains, there was a train running right down the middle of the avenue, only there weren't any crossings or traffic lights or anything and so these guys on horseback, these guys they called cowboys, they'd ride in front of the train, announcing the train was coming and clearing the way."

"No, I didn't know that," I tell her, stopping to let Rosa crop at some foliage.

"Yeah," Katie says wistfully, "it's true."

I lean over and kiss her then and she does that trick of sucking my lips into her mouth, like she's going to inhale my whole soul.

Being as she knows how to ride, I ask her if she wants to ride Rosa but she says not today. Soon, though. And her face gets bright at the prospect of it.

We walk my horse for a good hour, then put her away and go back to Katie's place and fuck some more. Finally, around 5 A.M., I go home, leaving Katie to sleep two hours before going to work.

When I got back to my apartment I sat in the orange chair and started freaking out a bit. I didn't know what I'd gotten myself into and I didn't like that.

So I didn't call Katie for three weeks. I unplugged my phone. I didn't go near A.A. meetings for fear I'd run into Laura or one of her friends, who would report spotting me to Katie.

I hadn't told Katie where I lived and I wasn't listed so she couldn't find me that way. I wasn't sure if she'd look but you never know.

I just sat home. With Kitten. I sent Eddie from the barn some money to take care of Rosa. In case Katie looked for me there. I only went out to shoplift at night.

My digestive problems got worse. It got to the point where I couldn't keep anything down. Finally I went to the Chinese doctor on Chatham Square.

He's a shriveled little guy with a long pointy beard. He's gotta be ninety. Doesn't speak a word of English. He feels all my pulses and has this young thug-looking kid translate his questions to me. After a while, the doctor scribbles out a bunch of stuff on a small scrap of paper that the thug guy hands to a third guy, who proceeds to mix up a big bag full of herbs and strange substances from jars on the counter.

When I emerge from the Chinese doctor's, I see Katie. She walks right by me, heading south, but not seeing me. I start to follow her. She turns onto Doyers Street.

She's so beautiful. Her long hair is trailing down her back and she has this amazing walk. My heart's beating fast. I want to overtake her and pin her against a wall and kiss her and fuck her, right there in the street, as the tight-lipped Chinese look away or maybe spit at the horror of White Devils displaying themselves like that.

I follow Katie over to Bayard Street, where she goes into a Thai restaurant. After a while I carefully peer in the window and see Katie sitting with crazy Laura at a table. I'm half tempted to just walk in there. Then I get a better idea: I could follow Katie around for a while, see what she does with herself. Maybe if it doesn't turn out she's fucking eight million other guys, maybe I'll call her and try to really get something going with her.

When Katie and Laura emerge from the Thai place, I follow.

They get in a cab. I get one too, and like I'm in a movie, I tell the driver, "Follow that cab."

They go to Laura's. She lives over in the West Village on Charles Street. I was there once, the time Laura fucked me.

I wait till I figure they're inside Laura's apartment, then I jimmy the lock on the downstairs door and go up to the second floor and put my ear to Laura's door to hear what they're talking about. But it's all muffled. I lose heart and go back outside and sit on a stoop to wait for Katie to come out of there. She emerges an hour later. I follow her. Onto the subway. The station is fairly deserted and I keep thinking she'll notice me but she's lost in her thoughts. I get on one car down from her. It's nerve-racking. Each time the train pulls into a stop I have to get up and check she hasn't gotten off—even though I'm fairly sure she's heading home.

Sure enough, she gets off at Forty-second and just goes home. Doesn't stop off at the store or anything. Once I've watched her go into her building, I head back for the subway and go downtown. I get home and I feel like a jerk, but just the same, all that next week I followed Katie. Although I'd gotten in the habit of bringing Kitten with me everywhere, I didn't bring her out for the Katie pursuit. I figured it'd draw too much attention and maybe Katie would cotton on to my tailing her.

I found out a lot about the girl. She worked down on Lower Broadway. Her boss was a Middle Eastern–looking guy who drove a white BMW. Once I followed the two of them all the way to the morgue. I didn't try to go into the morgue, though. I probably would have been stopped by morgue security, and besides, I was pretty sure Katie wasn't fucking her boss. They seemed to get along but I could tell from the way she held her body when she was near him that she wasn't interested in him.

At night, Katie either stayed in doing I'm not sure what or else hung out with a sort of odd-looking skinny girl who looked half Irish, half Nubian. Her and Katie would go get Chinese food and bring it back to Katie's. Sometimes a third girl would join them, a younger girl who looked enough like Katie that I figured she was her sister. The sister had two big white poodles, which seemed incongruous. The girl didn't look like a poodle type. Plus the dogs had something wrong with their legs; they walked like they were arthritic, this sort of stiff prancing gait. Actually, seeing Katie like that, walking down the street with the shorthaired girl, the sister, and the poodles, I really wanted to go say something to her. I mean, she just looked like a crackpot walking around with this posse of broken creatures. Not that the sister was broken. She was too young looking for that. But there was something slightly off about her. And the other girl looked like she might be a dyke. Maybe Katie was switch-hitting. But that didn't bother me. It didn't get me off or anything either. I don't have a big thing for girls doing other girls. Although I guess I wouldn't have minded watching Katie do it with a girl. I guess.

One night, Katie did go to the movies with a guy. I almost didn't follow her that night. Ever since I'd started my stakeout, I'd been missing classes left and right. So I'd planned on going to school, but then on a hunch went by Katie's. I'd only been watching her door twenty minutes when this small nervous-looking guy rang her bell. After a few minutes Katie popped out of her building all dolled up. Really beautiful, in a green dress with this off-white fake-fur coat. My heart was stammering. I followed them to Times Square, where they went into the movie *Titanic*. Which I found offensive. Just the notion of her going to that movie. Never mind with some loser weaselly-looking cretin. So I bought a ticket for fucking *Titanic* and sat a few rows behind Katie and the cretin to see if she was like going down on him or at least snuggling up to him. But she wasn't. The guy looked really stiff from what I could tell from the back of his little head. Even during the good part, when the boat's all topsy-turvy and everybody's falling off and dying, the guy's little head just remained stiff.

I almost lost them when they came out of the theater, but then, thanks to Katie's crazy coat, I found them again and followed.

Nothing happened, though. The guy walked Katie home and just pecked her on both cheeks and then walked off when she went inside her building.

So I buzzed her. She must have thought I was the cretin having forgotten to tell her something. She didn't even ask who it was over the intercom. Just buzzed me in.

And then there she is. Standing at the door with that face of hers all open and bright. For him, though. Not for me.

When she sees it's me, her mouth goes slack.

"Where'd you come from?" she says, knitting her little eyebrows.

"The street."

"Ah."

"Can I come in?"

"Now?"

"No, in a few hours. I'd like to sit in the hall for a while. Then let me in at one A.M. if you would."

She doesn't smile, though.

"You're not funny, Jack."

"No. I guess not. Listen, though," I say, then realize I'm not sure what I have to say.

"Yeah?"

"I've been sick. I'm sorry. I couldn't call."

"Ah," she says, not believing a word of it, cocking her hip and resting her bunched-up fist on it. What a darling fist she has. So small, yet utilitarian.

"You're so beautiful," I tell her and I honestly don't think

I've ever told anyone this because I've never really felt it. Even the time I was fucking the model, the Swiss girl who liked to be tied up. Everyone said she was beautiful but she didn't look that way to me.

"Um," Katie says, maybe warming an iota.

"Please, can I come in?"

"Laura's very worked up about that candle you gave her. Why do you go giving volatile girls candles with sexual invocations on them? You know how that can work on a girl's mind?" Katie says, frowning, chiding me, and isn't it my luck to have given Laura a sexual candle. I mean, what are the odds. Isn't Santeria based on Christianity and saints and whatnot?

"Laura's been losing sleep over it all 'cause she's tried to call you and never gets any answer. She's obsessed with you. I didn't tell her what happened with us."

"Jesus," I say, shaking my head. What the fuck.

"She's very sexy," Katie says then.

What is she, her pimp?

"Katie, come on, I'm not interested in her. I'm tired of psychos. Please, I just. . . . I'm sorry I didn't call you but I'll always call now. I'll always call. I'll do anything. Really. Please."

"But Jack, how do you know I want you to call? And what if I'm psycho? What if I'm going to tie you up and put Drano up your ass and call all my friends over to watch. You don't know, Jack. It's Russian roulette. Just 'cause I was nice once doesn't mean I always am."

"Of course. I know. You're right. Can I come in?"

"I guess."

I couldn't stay all night because I needed to feed Kitten. But I was there long enough for us to get reacquainted. She didn't put Drano up my ass but she fucked me nearly to death. I guess she was pretty angry and she took it out on my dick, and at one point did in fact tie me up, really seriously too, then blindfolded me and put ice cubes on my nipples and jerked me off with a leather glove on her hand.

"Where'd you learn all this stuff?" I asked her after she'd taken the blindfold off.

"What do you do for a living, Jack? Are you a criminal? Laura thinks you're a criminal."

"How many people have you fucked? Who taught you how to fuck like this?"

"Do you do burglaries, or what? You're not like a male hustler or something, are you?"

And so on. She didn't answer me and I didn't answer her but god did I love her. I guess I'd known it almost the moment I met her. And more the day I followed her through Chinatown. But definitely now. Feeling a little sick over whoever had taught her about sex. And about the cretin she had gone to the movies with. And about all the thoughts she could have that would exclude me.

Ten days later I'm sleeping at my place for the first night in more than a week. I feel like a stranger in here. Although now that I'm not hiding from Katie, I've gotten back into the swing of it all, back to taking Rosa for her walks, back to short cons and night classes, I don't feel like the guy that lived here. Something in Katie changed all that. Like a few days ago when she came out with me to the barn and expertly tacked Rosa up with a bridle and saddle she borrowed from Eddie. And then got on my horse while I walked alongside into the park. And then the look on Katie's face, her unbelievable happiness over being on a horse, her face lighting up so bright it hurt me.

And I'm a stranger now in my little low-ceilinged hovel. And it's hard sleeping in here, and no sooner do I finally fall asleep than I get woken by this awful sound. I stumble into the kitchen and don't you know, there's a fucking rat in the trash can again. Hurling himself against the sides. Angry.

So I call up Katie and tell her. How the rats are back and they're going to eat Kitten. She says come over and bring Kitten with me.

And I do.

And I just stay. I never even go back to get my orange chair or my comforter.

There's a bad moment when Laura finds out. She turns up on Katie's doorstep saying how she found me first. She's even clutching that stupid candle.

Katie ended up calling Laura's A.A. sponsor to come remove Laura. The sponsor said some kind of magic to Laura and the next time I ran into her, she just smiled primly and said a curt hello and that was it.

As for the intestinal thing, the vomiting and whatnot, it didn't exactly go away, but there's been a marked improvement.

TOOLS

I hadn't been feeling very well. The shrink was on me to come three times a week, but I didn't have that kind of money. Besides, I didn't think it'd do much good. He was a fairly inept shrink. He never said anything. Just listened as I blathered on. I don't know why I bothered.

I guess because of Elisa. She was big on that sort of thing. *Self-knowledge* was her favorite phrase. *There is no such thing as too much self-knowledge, Toby,* she would say to me sternly, all of it made so much more effectual by the outfit she had on. Usually a nice navy business suit. She was a lawyer. She still is a lawyer—although she has nothing to do with me anymore.

And maybe Elisa was right about the self-knowledge. I don't know. But at any rate, I was feeling low. My job was repulsive. My mother was dead. My forty-two-year-old sister, Vivian—a reformed-junkie electrician—was living in a trailer park in Tampa and was expecting a baby she'd conceived with her boyfriend, who was now in jail. Vivian had had to stop working as she's a clumsy electrician and was afraid she'd get shocked and electrocute her unborn child. And so she was broke. I sent money when I could, but that wasn't often. What with the shrink. And having gone into debt over Elisa's lingerie and champagne habit.

Elisa never even bothered to come pick up all that goddamned lingerie. Nor the children's books. The ones she'd make me read her when we played Baby-sitter. She'd lie in bed with her white cotton panties on under a nightgown. I'd sit at her side, reading nice stories. *Charlotte's Web. Where the Wild Things Are. Alice in Wonderland.* You know. And as I was reading, I'd start to make up things, adding to what was in the actual text. Maybe a vibrator stuck inside Charlotte's spiderweb. Or big dicks sprouting from the Wild Things' groins. Or I'd simply elaborate on the color of poor little Alice's nipples in Wonderland.

And Elisa would look up at me with those big brown eyes. "It doesn't say THAT," she would say, batting her lashes.

Once I went to watch Elisa in court. She's a prosecutor. I watched her grinding accusations at some hapless black kid who'd killed some other hapless black kid by pounding him over the head with a two-by-four. Elisa just made mincemeat of the defense. She looked so cold and taut there in the hideous fluorescent-lit courtroom, wearing navy pumps to match her suit, her black hair yanked up into this stern bun, and I just thought of the way her eyes grew round when I reached up her nightgown and read to her about Alice's wondrous tits.

Which is unfortunately an image I could not get out of my head. The roundness of Elisa's eyes.

We'd been engaged. We'd gone to look at real estate up in Westchester County. Hell. We'd picked out names for the kids. Julianna and Gregory. Then, one day, Elisa got it into her head that she wanted Judge Menson to read her bedtime stories instead of me.

"Toby," she'd said, reaching for my hand, "I'm sorry, but I'm in love with Herb Menson. I can't marry you."

She told me this over dinner one night at Bar Pitti. She was just dipping a hunk of bread into the small dish of olive oil. They serve the finest olive oil at that place. And even Elisa, who's a Nazi about her weight, would allow herself a dot of oil on her bread. And telling me she was in love with this crusty old judge didn't throw her off at all. She still dipped into the olive oil with extreme caution, imagining, no doubt, that just one extra iota of oil would render her instantly obese.

And that was that. After I'd paid for dinner and helped Elisa into her coat, she pecked me on the cheek and darted across Sixth Avenue. Maybe to get the subway up to Queens, where, I knew, Judge Menson lived in an enormous house, several rooms of which were overrun with his collections: antique judge's robes, surgical tools, and stamps, all lovingly displayed in glass cases. This fact reported to me by Elisa a few months earlier when she'd attended a cocktail party out there.

"What do you suppose the unifying thread in his collection is?" she'd asked me.

"Insanity," I'd said. At which she'd shrugged. Never letting on that she was getting a thing for the judge. That maybe she wanted to parade around modeling the judge's robes for him.

And so maybe that night on Sixth Avenue, after dumping me like that, maybe she went to catch the subway up to his place. And maybe they both wore robes as Judge Menson tucked Elisa into bed and started reading her children's books.

The thought of my former fiancée in bed in a dusty old black robe with some batty old judge reading her dirty bedtime stories made me profoundly sick.

So sick I called in sick for work the next day. And the day after that. And so on and so forth. I'd already been on shaky ground up there. I was an art director for corporate Web sites. And I had, I was told, an *attitude problem.* I was not a *team player.* But I was trying. I wanted it all to work out. With the job. With Elisa. The house. The kids. The whole bit. I wanted to go that route.

I'd come up dirt poor in Tampa, Florida, but even though my mother was an alcoholic, my sister was a junkie, and my brother was a criminal, I'd stayed fairly straight. Went to college. Was adept with computers and design. Screwed around doing layout and some editorial stuff for local papers and got in on the whole Web thing. Then, three years ago, when I found out my girlfriend at the time—this go-go dancer I'd rescued from total depravity—was turning tricks, I almost lost it. I started to feel very backed into a corner. Like no matter what I did, I was still Toby Smith, born in a trailer park, raised by a foulmouthed drunk, and endlessly a magnet for runaways, strippers, would-be presidential assassins, and volunteers for chemical castration. In a word: loser.

So I moved to New York. By then I was already thirty though, so I was ancient as far as Web designing was concerned. I ended up having to bartend for a while and then, finally, getting desperate to pay the rent on my Chelsea hovel, accepted my brother George's offer to drive a shipment up from Florida. Pot. Lots of it. A goddamned Mack truck full of it. You can bet I was sweating bullets. George had had the foresight to steal a bunch of Valiums from his girlfriend's stash, and although I hate those kinds of things, I ended up eating them like candy just to make it. By the time I'd gotten the load into Brooklyn and safely into the guy's driveway out in Gravesend, I'd lost ten pounds and a lot of emotional stability. The guy I brought the shipment to was a total freak, a quarterback-sized Russian with a tattooed face, wouldn't let me come in his house to freshen up or anything, and I was too shaky and fucked up to hike over to the subway, so I made the guy call me a car service and I sat there on his god-damned lawn with a bunch of plastic pink flamingos stuck in it. And the guy just stood on his porch, looking at me, like maybe I was gonna fuck with his lawn or his flamingos. Eventually the car service got there and took me home to Manhattan. But it all showed me I was just not cut out for this kind of activity. The next day I pounded the pavement like crazy. I must have gone on fifty interviews over the next week, and finally it happened. I got a Web site designing job in this big bland high-rise in midtown. I had a helluva time getting it together clothingwise, but I'm good at what I do and they saw that and, begrudgingly, respected it and didn't bother me too much. In the meantime, I met Elisa. At a coffee bar on Seventh Avenue. She was standing next to me, putting cream in her coffee. She asked if I didn't think the coffee quality was falling off lately.

I just stammered something like, "Uh, yeah, maybe," or some other ineffectual comeback, because women in suits, although profoundly arousing, scare the shit out of me, and god did she have a suit on.

She beamed a smile at me, a smile that stayed with me. And when I saw her in the coffee place a few days later, I fumbled out some attempt at a come-on and she rounded her eyes and said, "Oh, are you asking me out?" and I admitted that I guessed I was and she smiled then and said, "Okay, yes, let's do something."

She had tickets to an off-Broadway play the next night and so we went to that. It involved this woman wandering around in a nightgown and a guy who was drunk. It was a Mike Leigh play and I didn't know of him at the time, but thanks to Elisa, now I've rented all the movies he's made and even though these are too gritty and true to be a release from life—the way I like movies to be—they are nonetheless amazing movies.

During the play I kept looking at the outline of Elisa's knees, draped by the fabric of her long tan skirt. Maybe it was the way that material fell over her knees, I don't know, but I got more forward than is my custom. I mean, ordinarily, the type of women I attract are predators, tearing into me right away. Elisa was a little aloof, though. I couldn't quite read her. But that tan fabric on her knees did me in, and although she demurred about coming over to my place, I was incredibly persuasive.

A little later I had her in there, within the walls of my two-room hovel. I reached for her hips. She just stood there, intimidating the shit out of me. Not only was she aloof, but she was a completely different breed from my usual trailer park fare. But I forced myself to act the way I figured all my predecessors had acted: supremely self-confident. I started undoing the little fake pearl buttons of her striped blouse. Slowly. Trying to get her worked up. Until I got her bra off. Then I lost control over her nice round tits with large nipples that made me feel like a rutting animal. I went nuts on her pleasing curved physique. And was a nervous wreck the next day, at work, after Elisa had left my place in the middle of the night, not waking me, and leaving a little note that just said, "Bye, Toby," which I didn't know how to interpret but then figured out when she called me that night and asked me to come over.

I quickly came to understand what Elisa liked: to be passive and malleable and have me read her dirty bedtime stories. This was a new one on me. The women I'd known were bossy both in life and in bed. But I guess Elisa got her domineering streak out in the courtroom. In bed, she wanted me to prosecute. Pretty early on, say two weeks into our thing, I was over at her place and she showed me this shelf of children's books.

"I love to be read to," she told me, pulling out a copy of *Babar.*

"Oh yeah?" I said, not getting it at first, a little startled to see this supremely together chick telling me she liked to have children's stories read to her.

"Read to me?" she asked, making her eyes big.

"Okay." I shrugged.

"Wait," she told me, then went in her bedroom for a minute and reemerged into the living room wearing a frilly white nightgown. She lay down on the couch and I started reading to her from *Babar*. After a few sentences, she said, "But isn't there more to it than that?" And I didn't get it. I shook my head no.

"But isn't Babar horny?" she asked innocently. And finally it clicked. And pretty soon I was turning those children's books into utter filth.

Once she was all worked up from the readings, I would tie her up with silk restraints, tether her in the kitchen or the bathroom, and tease the hell out of her. Torture her. The way she did the criminals in the courtroom. I prosecuted her body. She never asked me to, of course. But I had good instincts with her. So I'd tether her. Flick my tongue at different parts of her. She would try not to betray arousal but involuntary quivers would shake her hips and make her mouth twitch. When we were both ready to lose it, finally, I'd go down on her savagely or fuck her as hard as I'd ever fucked anyone.

So we got along well. Pretty soon I forgot that I was white trash and she was not.

One night, Elisa was lying in my bed, in a yellow nightie. I was reading *Where the Wild Things Are*. As I read to her, her eyes got even bigger than usual and she whispered that she loved me. I just pressed on with *Babar* for a minute and then reached for her round tits under the nightgown and told her I loved her. Remarkably, this didn't make her wince or have an emotional meltdown like it had past girlfriends.

Next thing I knew, I'd asked Elisa to marry me and her eyes got big and she said "Yes" and I went into debt getting her a ring from a jewelry store in Soho. By then we were together a year and a half and I guess I started getting confident, thinking she was in for the long haul and that I'd finally shed my past and was heading toward a nice life like I'd always wanted.

So when she dumped me that night at Bar Pitti, even though I tried not to let on, I was devastated. I'd kind of thought I'd been taking it easy, not making an enormous emotional investment in her, since I'd been burned so many times. I thought that in spite of our having looked at real estate and my having met her parents—who were going to help finance the house—and in spite of having come up with names for the kids and even discussed what kind of dog we might like to get, I thought I'd kept a degree of distance, a somewhat take-it-or-leave-it attitude.

I realized that just wasn't the case at all as I watched her jaywalk across Sixth Avenue. I felt awful. I made it back up to my place in one piece, but then I just couldn't move and, like I said, kept calling in sick for work and eventually told them I'd contracted pneumonia and would be out for a long time. For some reason they didn't fire me. One coworker even sent a *Get Well Soon* card, and although at first I showed up for the shrink—he actually had a hard time repressing his delight at this crisis, which I guess he thought would engender some sort of huge psychological breakthrough—after a week I just stopped going. I didn't call to cancel, nor did I return his messages when he called me, and I guess I was racking up a big bill with him as he had a twenty-four-hour cancellation policy, and finally, after two weeks, I left a message saying I wouldn't be back, I was moving out of town.

The only place I was moving, though, was from one side of my bed to the other. Once in a while I would go out. I rerented all the Mike Leigh movies. This was a mistake as these movies did anything but cheer me. But I was taking perverse pleasure in the hideous foibles of the working-class Brits, their horrible lives addled with anorexia and poverty and drinking, and it got so I could understand their incredibly strong Cockney accents and I even started thinking in Cockney and really feeling like I was living in a Mike Leigh movie, and then one night, I was going to rent *Life Is Sweet* for the fourth time, but something drew me to the David Cronenberg shelf. I'd seen some of his movies but not *Crash,* and although I knew I ought to be renting things that would cheer me, like Tim Burton movies that have definite diabolical undertones but ultimately are so brightly colored that they can't help but cheer you, I rented *Crash* and I guess that was my big mistake. I mean, god, did that one depress me and furthermore remind me of Elisa, who of course wasn't into mangling herself for sexual kicks, but the Rosanna Arquette character reminded me of her a little: this twisted outward innocence masking the core of a true pervert. And this is what got me thinking about doing something to myself. Like altering my consciousness somehow to take me out of my misery, to engender a new experience, anything. I'd been around way too many drug addicts to find that route appealing and I guess I could have gone out to get a hooker but I'd probably end up having *feelings* for her because she'd likely remind me of my ex–go-go dancer/whore girlfriend from Florida, all of which would sink me down lower and I didn't exactly want to get in a car crash, not that I had a car to get in a crash with anyway, but self-mutilation started to have its appeal and it began pretty mildly, just cutting myself on the stomach and the arms, standing in front of the mirror, watching the blood bubble up on the lips of the little incisions I made, and it definitely was in some way altering my consciousness and I stopped eating and even stopped watching movies and got into this state, this sort of extended lucid dream, where I would just walk around in tight circles, stopping now and then in front of the mirror to cut myself, and

And I don't know how the hell I end up at Bellevue since my hovel is much closer to St. Vincent's but that's where I am, at Bellevue, and right away this intern puts a sponge to my throat and tells me, "Hold on a minute," like I'm going somewhere, and then another intern comes along and looks at me and says he's going to get some clamps.

When the clamp intern comes back, he tells the first guy to let up on the pressure.

"But, Norm, if I let up he'll shoot blood all over everything."

"No, Alan, I don't think he got his carotids. Look at him, he's very conscious," he says.

And I try to say something to agree with this diagnosis but all I can do is make gurgling sounds and then the first guy lets up on the pressure and they clamp off my veins, then wheel me off to an operating room, where, they tell me, they're going to clean up my wound and put sutures in—which all sounds like a reasonable course of action, and I gurgle an "Okay."

When I come to, I'm on the flight deck. Imagine. Little ol' me, Toby Smith from Tampa, in the psych ward at Bellevue. In a straitjacket, no less—which I discover when I try to get up to go to the bathroom. My mind is working fine but my arms are strapped down to my chest under the thick white cloth of the jacket. There's a nurse's call button on the wall but it's not like I can reach it.

Eventually a very wide nurse waddles into the room. She is darkest black and has an out-of-control Afro, not the sort of tidy restrained hairdo you expect in a nurse.

"Ah, Mister Smith," she says, surprising me with a beautifully lilting Caribbean accent, "I see you're awake."

"I would like to go to the bathroom," I tell her, finding that

I can speak although my throat still feels pretty fucking weird.

"Yes. Of course," she says and reaches under my bed, producing a yellow plastic bedpan, and I take a moment to note this color, the color of urine, and wonder at the psychological thoughts of the bedpan manufacturer's design squad, and I have no intention of mingling my urine with the urine yellow plastic of the bedpan. "I mean, I'd like to go into an actual bathroom, please," I tell the nurse just as a doctor materializes at my bedside. A female doctor. A very fine-looking female doctor.

"I'm sorry we've had to restrain you, Mister Smith, but we don't want you doing yourself any more harm," the doctor tells me. "Do you remember, Mister Smith, what happened?"

She has pulled a chair over to my bedside and the nurse has wedged the bedpan under me and although the bedpan is under the sheet, I absolutely cannot take a leak with this good-looking lady doctor here, gently lifting her skinny eyebrows that I think are penciled in because she's a redhead and I seem to recollect from somewhere, redheads have red eyebrows and, yes, red pubic hair too, and these eyebrows are brown, but she's a very lovely doctor, really. She has a little upturned nose and skin as white as a snake's belly.

"I had a bit of an accident with a steak knife," I say. "Uh . . . Doctor Ray," I add, reading her I.D. tag, on which is a fine little photo of her—because she's the type of woman who can even look good in those sorts of photos.

"That's a nice euphemism, Mister Smith. An accident with a steak knife. I suppose you were just doing the dishes and it jumped out of the sink and attacked your throat?"

"Pretty much, yeah," I say, grinning, pleased to find a doctor with a sense of humor. "You can call me Toby, Doctor Ray."

"Fine, then. Toby. Now. Tell me a little about yourself, Toby, if you wouldn't mind."

"Not at all, Doctor Ray," I say, and I tell her a little about myself, but talking fast because I need to take a leak so bad, and about fifteen minutes into it, she's telling me I can call her Jody, and I'm thinking she's spending an inordinate amount of time with me, because I've only been hospitalized once for a severe broken leg when I was twenty and dove off a bridge and didn't crack my head open but did end up banging the lower half of my body against the end of a boat that happened to zip under the bridge as I dove, and although it was quite a fracture, requiring three weeks of traction, the doctors only ever made the most perfunctory visits, but maybe it's something to do with being in the psych ward, maybe once you're far gone enough to warrant this ward you also get a lot more attention.

And finally, to the relief of my bladder, Dr. Jody Ray leaves, and I piss into the bedpan, then have to sit there with it under my ass for about two hours before a different nurse comes in and removes the bedpan and also gives me a bunch of pills and I sleep for quite a long time.

The next day, I don't know what's become of Dr. Jody Ray—who at least was kind enough to leave orders for my straitjacket to be removed today—and I've shuffled around the ward a bit but I haven't seen any doctors all day long, just my fellow nuts, most of them in really very sad shape and one guy, this old white guy, discoursing at me about Kant and Heidegger and even Plato as we sit together in the TV room watching soap operas where the people look like no people I've ever seen or would ever want to see and then suddenly the guy, who's in the middle of a tangent as he stares at some surgically altered beast of a woman onscreen, suddenly he shoots up out of his chair and races over to the big window, beating his fists against it, imploring, "LET ME IN, LET ME IN," like he's asking the sky to let him in.

Late at night, about 10 P.M. or so, the last time on earth you'd expect to see a doctor, this little furtive-looking guy with a hook nose and burning black eyes turns up at my bedside. He's a very distracted-looking individual who introduces himself as Dr. Wool and makes me recount my whole story for him. This makes me wonder if Jody Ray failed to make any notes on my case or maybe was actually an apparition or something because she did seem too good to be true.

Dr. Wool is really a very odd person. He's nervous but drunk-seeming at the same time, and at various points while I'm telling my story, he bursts out in a hiccuping little laugh over things that I would not have thought funny, like Elisa dumping me over dinner and darting across Sixth Avenue, and Dr. Wool keeps leaning too close to me and his black eyes really look like the eyes of a complete maniac. Then, just as I'm telling him about renting *Crash*—which, of course, he has a field day with once I tell him it involves people getting in car crashes for sexual kicks—one of my roommates, a tall black guy who I think is a Vietnam vet and has had periodic outbursts when no one is around—but is well behaved when nurses and doctors appear—he suddenly leaps out of bed and starts screaming and pulling at his hair that already has some bald patches and he's doing this wild sort of dance, his long limbs like jubilant matchsticks, and Dr. Wool and I are just staring at him. Although Dr. Wool, I'm sure, should be doing something, he is just looking over, with his eyes growing bigger, and finally he pats me on the hand. "Just a moment, Mister Smith," he says, then gets up, pushes my nurse call button, and goes over to the dancing black guy.

"Sir," Dr. Wool says, standing about a foot in front of the guy. "Sir."

But the black guy keeps doing his wild dance until suddenly he topples forward, screaming and clutching his stomach, and I sit up higher in my own bed to better observe all this as a massive dark stain blossoms on the front of the black guy's gown.

Dr. Wool is bending over him, lifting up the gown, and it's basically the most hideous thing I've ever seen in my life. The guy has a wound under there and he's evidently popped all the stitches. His insides are pouring forth, blood and intestines and just much more gore than you would think one abdomen could contain, and meanwhile the guy's long thin dick is just hanging there, bathed in all this blood, just a lifeless thing that has long forgotten its glories and conquests.

Finally a nurse appears and summons more nurses and doctors and pretty soon we've got all hell breaking loose and the four other nuts in our room are awake, all of them arisen from their torpors to witness the self-evisceration of the black guy, and finally I can't take it anymore, I've seen enough, and I pull the little privacy curtain around my bed and hum to myself, until eventually one of the nurses comes to administer an additional shot and I slip off to the land of nod.

Things are greatly improved the next day when Jody Ray appears at my bedside. "Did you miss me?" she asks, tilting her head at me, and if I wasn't in a nuthouse, I would swear she was flirting with me, and I tell her, "Hell, yeah, I missed you. And when, by the way, am I getting out of this place?" And she pats my hand, letting her own hand linger there, on top of mine, longer than seems necessary, and says, "Any day now, Toby, any day. We just have to get you on the right medication and then you can go. Why? You in a hurry to leave me?"

I tell her I'm certainly not in a hurry to leave her—but neither am I big on medications of any sort. Yet each time I demur over the Zoloft, Jody Ray adds another day onto my stay, so finally I agree that I'll go on it, and, yes, come for outpatient visits with Dr. Wool, although, I tell her, I would have preferred outpatient with her, but she smiles this funny smile and tells me that that wouldn't be a good idea, and finally it dawns on me a few days later, when I'm at home, why it isn't a good idea for me to have Jody Ray as a shrink.

I've had a helluva time at home, what with picking up all the detritus that accumulated during my slump and then showing up back at work, where, in my absence, they just let everything accumulate and there is so much mindless crap for me to do that I nearly feel another slump coming on and, yes, almost have an urge to cut myself. I pull through it, though, and begin to methodically attack the workload. I haven't been taking the Zoloft, because I believe the hospitalization alone rearranged my brain chemistry, shook some things up and helped me deal with the loss of Elisa. I've managed to call my poor sister, Vivian—who's about to give birth at any second—and I've also made contact with the friends I have, and now, when the phone rings and I answer and this pretty voice comes at me, right away, I know it's her.

"Have you thought about me at all, Toby?" she says, knowing that I'll know it's her.

"I've thought about you a great deal, Jody," I tell her.

"That's good, because I'm planning to cook us dinner tonight and it wouldn't do to make dinner for someone who hadn't thought of me."

I am silent for a moment because this comes so far from left field that it knocks the wind out of me.

"Are you there?"

"I am," I say, still a little breathless.

"Good. Shall we say eight o'clock, then?"

"Sure," I say, and when I've gotten the address, I put the phone back in its cradle and stare ahead, dumbfounded. I mean, the way she sounded, it definitely seemed like she had impure intentions, like this was a date or something, but surely it can't be. This must just be some perverse form of therapy. Or else she's nuts. Either way, though, I'm pretty curious, and so, when the time comes, I shower and dress carefully, going so far as to put on newish underwear.

She doesn't live far from me, on Twenty-second Street close to Tenth Avenue, in a beautiful brownstone. I ring the bell marked Ray. The door buzzes and I go up one flight, where Jody is waiting in the hallway. The breath gets knocked right out of me. She's wearing a slinky dress of dark green with tiny straps and her red hair is lustrous, falling just below her chin, and for a moment she reminds me of the redhead in the Cronenberg movie *Dead Ringers,* only Jody's narrower than that woman, much more acrobatic looking and filled with nervous energy as she offers a simple smile and shows me in.

The place is amazing, very quirky but beautiful with old lamps, dark wood, and slumpy velvet furnishings. The lighting is dim and it's like a combination of a study and an opium den, you feel that at any moment twelve languorous women, each slinkier than the next, will pour forth, melting through the walls to wrap themselves around you. But Jody doesn't wrap herself around me, just takes my hand and leads me into what I suppose is the dining room—although I soon discover it's hard to distinguish which room is which, they are all draped and cushiony with lounging surfaces and muted Old World tones. Clearly, though, the last room she shows me is the bedroom. It sports a cast iron bed and I wonder if she's just going to throw me down on it, but no, she leads me back into the dining room and there is a long dark wood table with blue plates and glasses and Jody tells me to sit, she'll be right back, and then she goes into the kitchen for a minute, soon emerging with platters of beautiful food.

It's quite a meal and quite a conversation, with Jody asking me how I've been making out in the exterior world, making sure I made it to my outpatient appointment with Dr. Wool, which of course I did, and which of course was an exercise in bizarreness, what with him coming in ten minutes late looking like he'd just stumbled out of a whorehouse, and when, a few days ago, I spoke with my sister, Vivian, she was rather insistent that I go back to my former shrink, a psychoanalyst as opposed to a psychiatrist, because analysis is how she, Vivian, has managed to stay off heroin and electrocute herself only minimally in both the metaphoric and literal senses in spite of living in a trailer park and having a horrible life, and when I relay all this to Jody, she frowns slightly, her lovely little drawn-on eyebrows pulling together.

"Yes. Analysis. The talking cure. Yes. A wonderful tool. But I hope you've been taking your Zoloft, Toby."

"Actually, really, no, I haven't," I say, realizing I'm blowing my chances for getting laid—but feeling strongly enough about my own half-baked theories of brain chemistry to tell Jody the truth.

"You haven't?" she says, holding her fork full of salmon halfway between her plate and her lovely mouth.

"No, Jody, I haven't. It's like my Bellevue experience jarred me out of my slump, evened out my brain chemistry, if you will, and so, no, I haven't taken the Zoloft and I think antidepressants have this tendency to make everything even-keel, which is not something I'm interested in."

"Oh," she says, studying the pink fish on her fork and then finally putting it in her mouth and chewing thoughtfully.

"Please don't take it personally," I say, worried she's going to kick me out on the spot. "I'm not trying to disparage your professional opinion or anything."

"No," she says, but now she's playing with her food, like the fact of my not taking my Zoloft has killed off her appetite. "But you surprise me, Toby."

"How so?"

"You have strong opinions."

"That's surprising?" I say, insulted.

"I didn't mean it that way. Only that it's uncommon to meet someone in your situation with as much awareness as you seem to have."

"Oh," I say, pissed off. She might as well tell me I'm white trash scum and, as such, not entitled to know my brain from a rat's ass.

"You're upset," she says.

"I'm furious," I say, staring at her as I slowly rise from my chair.

"But you mustn't be. You've been bad. You've gone against doctor's orders," she says, her tone switching now, turning sexual, the whole feel of the room metamorphosizing from austere to boudoir as Jody starts to get this look in her blue eyes, this crazy burning look. I'm standing up now and her eyes are going over me in an incredibly appraising way, sizing me up and mentally undressing me. She pushes her plate away, stands up, wipes her mouth with her napkin, then comes to stand in front of me.

"Jody," I say then, "I'm not sure if I'm entirely comfortable with this situation."

"Comfort has little to do with anything," she says, then reaches up and digs her hands into my shoulders, like she's giving me a particularly vicious shoulder rub.

At first, I figure I'm experiencing just another notch in my belt of weird experiences with the good-looking but ultimately insane women I frequently attract. Then it turns out there's a little more to it.

Jody is indeed sexually manic. She pushes me down onto the floor and tears my pants off and starts to blow me like you wouldn't believe, so precisely that I have to yank her mouth off me so I don't shoot off right away. And she seems to quite like it when I make her put on a nightgown and get into bed, and I sit there talking dirty to her. And it is then, in that moment, as she looks up at me with those rather large but somewhat dead blue eyes, that I glimpse something. Which is very unfortunate, for these are the sorts of glimpses that invariably lead to love. What I see is a bit of her that is scared and soft and sadistic at once, and you take someone that screwed up and arm them with this amazing physique, a lovely face, and a medical degree, and you've got no end of trouble, which is what I feel coming on as I leave her place at the crack of dawn, as she gets ready to go to the hospital, as she gives me a sweet kiss goodbye and sends me off into the world.

I keep showing up for my appointments with Dr. Wool, and although I don't name names, I tell him someone has come into my life. A woman who is sexually insatiable and intelligent and good looking and I have no idea what she wants me for, and Dr. Wool seems to puzzle over it too but says, "Well, Toby, these things that come into our life, these situations, these people, although we're sometimes at a loss as to why they've come, in the end, we find that they are tools, Toby, tools for making a ladder and climbing, Toby."

Dr. Wool punctuates every few words with my first name like that, I guess to try and seem more personable, for he's really not a personable guy at all.

After six weeks my outpatient stint ended, and to my surprise, things with Jody kept going. In fact, it started reaching a level I never anticipated. One night we were having sex, actually very sedate sex, and Jody just started melting. Her face bunched up and sobs came out of her—which was interesting to feel from the perspective of being inside her.

"What? Did I hurt you? Jody? What is it?" I asked, looking into her eyes that still, for all the things that had started flowing between us, had a deadness in them.

Jody just kept sobbing, though. For quite some time. Finally she said it hadn't been like this in so long, she hadn't been able to have remotely ordinary sex with anyone in so long, because she hated everybody and it was just this thing, this thing where she had to come and had to come in as many ways as possible, as inventively as possible, but now, with me, somehow it was different.

I wasn't sure how to interpret this but I knew Jody had a pretty weird sexual history, a pretty weird history, period: wealthy psychiatrist parents who'd long stopped talking to her, then died in a plane crash and left her, their only child, all their money and a huge house in Rye, New York, that Jody to this day leaves sitting there, empty and falling to shambles. Over the years, Jody had jumped from one man to the next, a lion tamer to a lawyer to an actor to a woman to a painter and so on, staying with each one for a shorter time and always having weird encounters in sex clubs and sometimes even with hookers and yes, Jody was doubtless a little off the map sexually but it did seem like our bodies communicated well and by now, certainly, I loved her, and when she sobbed in my arms, it broke me in two and wrapped me around her finger.

A week after that, my sister, Vivian, had her baby. From what Viv told me, it wasn't a pretty picture, what with Vivian being very petite and rather old to be having a first baby, and there was an endless and painful labor culminating in a C-section. Vivian was in the hospital for four days before she and little Jenny Anne went home to the trailer park. Jody and I decided to go down and visit Vivian. She had no one. Neither Viv nor I speak to our brother George anymore and of course Jenny Anne's father was doing five years for armed robbery.

Jody and I had never been on a plane together and so, to celebrate the occasion, we fucked in the bathroom. It was good-natured animalistic sex like we'd had in the beginning, before all the emotions started crowding our physical interactions. I propped Jody's ass on that tiny sink and hoisted her skirt up and then fit myself inside her. I held her hips tightly but she slipped and I guess her shoe hit the flush button and the toilet made that incredible sucking sound those things make. Jody and the toilet moaned at the same moment, which of course made me laugh right as I came and so I was laughing and coming and Jody was flushing and coming and I guess we'd been in there a while and made a bit of a racket, for when we emerged everyone on the plane stopped what they were doing and just stared at us. Jody straightened her skirt and swooshed down the narrow aisle, hips first.

We got a cab from the Tampa airport to the Campland Trailer Park, where Vivian lived. The cab's AC was broken and the hot Florida air stuck to us as we drove down the freeway, passing strip malls and condo complexes, all of it pale and wavering in the heat.

The cab pulled into the park and stopped in front of number 67, a nondescript beige trailer. I paid the driver and got out. I didn't know how Jody would react to a trailer park but she seemed thrilled as she climbed out of the cab, straightened her skirt, and looked around.

"What nice palm trees," she said, gesturing at some sad palms planted between Viv's trailer and the next one over.

"Have you ever been to Florida before?" I asked, realizing I didn't know.

"Sure," she said, but she didn't volunteer when, how, or why, so I left her to admiring the palm trees and knocked on Vivian's door.

In a moment the door flew open and what I assumed was my sister appeared. Her dirty-blonde hair had turned mostly white and her face was skeletal, making her intense blue eyes stand out all the more. Before throwing her arms around my neck, she smiled at me and I saw she'd lost a tooth in her travels. Not the frontmost tooth, but still. She looked like she was sixty, not forty-two. I was horrified. At the world for doing this to her, at myself for not intervening. As I hugged her to me, I heard the baby start to cry inside the trailer. Vivian pulled away from me and went back in to the baby. I turned to Jody. "Come on." I motioned for her to follow me in.

Vivian had all the curtains drawn for some reason and it was very dark. When my eyes adjusted, I saw that Viv had the baby in her arms.

"This is Jenny Anne," Vivian said, offering me the little bundle, "and I take it you're Jody," she said sweetly, smiling at my girlfriend.

"Yes, I am, hello," Jody said, pleasantly enough, but I could sense she was freaked out. My sister looked like a maniac and the baby was dressed in the weirdest getup: a little red knit cap, pink T-shirt, no pants or diapers, and strange green booties that came all the way up to her knees.

"I was just about to put a new diaper on her," Vivian said, reassuring me that at least she wasn't letting the infant excrete indiscriminately all over the house. "You two make yourselves at home," she said, motioning at a filthy green sofa. "That there couch pulls out into a bed. That's where you'll be sleeping."

Jody and I looked at each other and I could just picture it, our getting on one of our irrepressible fuck jags and Jody wanting me to tie her up and then go at her from behind so hard I might ram her head into the back of the couch and the thing would suddenly fold up and close us inside it like some monstrous man-eating plant.

"Oh, Viv, no, we're not gonna put you out like that. We made a reservation at the Holiday Inn."

"You know you didn't have to do that," Vivian said, but I could tell she was sort of relieved.

"However you're most comfortable, though." Viv shrugged just as the baby started crying again. Vivian, never a bashful one to begin with, whipped out her tit, but the baby evidently wanted something else and kept on sobbing, and next thing I knew, Jody had started crying right along with the baby, and as Vivian and I both stared at her, Jody got up and rushed out of the trailer.

Vivian and I looked at each other and for a moment there was that thing, that brother-and-sister bond that no amount of time or distance can take away. It was me and her against the world, but right now my world had Jody in it and so I followed her outside.

She was standing there, leaning against the side of the trailer, sobbing. I put my hands on her shoulders. "Jody, what is it?" I asked, trying to get her to look at me.

"It's the baby, Toby, the baby."

And I thought, Oh no, Jody's biological clock is ticking, fuck me. But immediately Jody dissuaded me of this notion.

"I don't mean I want a baby or I'm freaked out by Vivian's baby. I mean there already is a baby. There is Gabriel. My baby."

"You have a baby?"

"My old girlfriend had a baby with my ex-boyfriend and for a while I lived with her, with Millicent, and with the baby, but Millicent was awful, she's old and she's really getting senile, and now I never see the boy. And I love that boy."

"Come again?" I said, totally bewildered, and then Jody explained some utterly bizarre situation whereby one of her boyfriends had impregnated this woman Millicent, a forty-seven-year-old lesbian Jody had been having an affair with, and Millicent wanted the baby, and this engendered fuzzy feelings in Jody. And so, Jody and Millicent raised the baby. Jody went to med school and supported the little family with money from her dead parents. Eventually they even got a little place upstate. And all was well until Jody went looking for sex outside the home, and although Jody didn't think it was relevant, Millicent went nuts over it all and got a restraining order so Jody couldn't come near her or Gabriel. And that's where it stood.

I didn't know quite what to say. So I asked Jody to marry me. I got down on my knees, there in the Campland Trailer Park on Nebraska Avenue, not too far from the trailer park where I'd been raised, and asked my unstable but lovable girlfriend to marry me.

"It'd be great, Jody. Maybe we can adopt the kid. Get a house. A dog."

"Toby, you shock me."

"I do?"

"The last time you got engaged you ended up at Bellevue, remember?"

"Vividly yes. And I met you. And I want to be with you."

"Oh," she said, frowning a little, then looking around her.

"Okay," she said then, shrugging.

"Okay what?"

"Let's get married."

"Really?"

"Let's do it. Now."

"Now?"

"Well. We'll get a license. That'll take a couple of days. But then Vivian can give you away."

"I don't think I need to be given away."

"Sure you do. Come on, we're being rude to your sister," Jody said then, suddenly completely reconstituted. She took my hand and led me back into Vivian's trailer.

My sister was contentedly feeding the baby and her eyes were milked over with a motherhood look that was the last thing I'd ever expect from my sister, who as a teenager had so many abortions she practically had a standing account at the Tampa Planned Parenthood. But this was a new Vivian. The years of heartbreaks and abuses were on her face and had aged her a great deal, but there was also something new about her, an undiluted bliss.

A little later, Jody and I took Vivian to dinner. Although Jody had thoughtfully looked up interesting Tampa restaurants before coming, Vivian wanted to be taken to IHOP. No matter what we said Vivian just shook her head. "I need to go to IHOP."

And so, we got the baby in her car seat, piled into my sister's creaky old Honda, and drove to the IHOP. The baby nested in her carrier and Vivian barely took her eyes off Jenny Anne long enough to take small bites of blintzes. She did pay attention, though, when I told her Jody and I were going to get married. And of course Vivian broke into a fit of that crazy laugh of hers when I told her Jody had been one of my doctors at Bellevue and that's how we met.

"Oh, Toby," Vivian said when her laugh had died down enough for her to speak, "I'd expect nothing less of you, baby brother," and she reached over and, very uncharacteristically, tweaked my cheek.

After dinner, Vivian dropped us off at the Holiday Inn overlooking the freeway and Jody and I ripped into each other.

Now that we were engaged, there was yet another layer to things and it was one I liked. The idea that this woman was going to actually marry me. A rich girl. A doctor. A maniac. We fucked on the floor. It had maroon carpet and I got rug burns on my knees.

Two days later, we got married. Vivian had found us a place called the Merry Chapel of Love. It was a house set a ways back from the road. The yard was addled with sinister plaster cherubs and there was this crazy Baroque fountain in the middle of the lawn. Vivian, carrying the baby in a papooselike thing on her stomach, led the way down the path to the front door.

A fat blonde woman opened the door and told us the Lord welcomed us to his house.

"And so do we," she added coyly as she ushered us inside. She introduced herself as Samantha, the preacher's wife. She was wearing a Hawaiian-print housedress that stopped right at her very small feet.

The room we were in was unbelievable. I guess it had been their living room but they had it done up like a whorehouse chapel: red velvet carpet on the little aisle between the three rows of pews, a sort of altar with a huge velvet painting of Jesus smiling benevolently, and the ceiling dripping with candelabras finished off in faux gold leaf.

Jody and I looked at each other. We'd intended to tie the knot at the courthouse but Vivian had insisted we be married by a proper preacher.

I don't know how proper this guy was, though. He came loping out of a side room and beamed a huge smile at us. "Welcome my children," he said—although he looked younger than me and Jody. He had long brown hair pulled into a slimy ponytail and when he smiled, I saw that he had millions of teeth. Really an inordinate amount of very small teeth. I shook his hand.

"This is the entire wedding party?" the wife asked now. She

looked very sad when Jody told her it was. This sadness compounded when we told her that, yes, we were ready and, no, we weren't changing into "something fancier."

A few minutes later, as the preacher evangelically recited his shtick, my sister started sobbing. For a moment, it occurred to me to bolt. To just turn around and race out into the hot Florida day and maybe find a bar and get drunk with some old guys. To get away from all this sobbing. The last twenty-four hours there'd been nothing but sobbing females. Did I really want an entire life of this?

But it passed. After all, it wasn't Jody that was sobbing. It was my crazy sister. I turned around at one point and saw she had a veritable river of snot flowing out of her. I suppose all this was pushing her buttons. She'd never been married, and although I'd never thought she wanted to, I hadn't thought she wanted a kid either.

Afterward, when Jody and I were officially married, after we'd kissed a nice deep kiss and I'd wished I could bend her over one of the empty pews and enter her from behind, the preacher wanted to get chatty. He was in a Christian rock band and wanted to tell us all about it. I tried to feign interest but then, fortunately, little Jenny Anne started crying and we all hightailed it out of there.

Jody, I guess, slipped Vivian a check to help out until Vivian could start working again and Jody didn't tell me this until we were back in New York, in my hovel, with Jody making a fuss over my wanting to bring any of my stuff over to her apartment.

"Jody, I don't want you giving my sister money. That's my job. She's my sister."

"No. She's my sister too now. I can give her money."

"I don't want it to be like that. I don't want you running the show. You're smarter than me and you're richer than me, but please try not to rub it in."

"What can I rub then?" my wife asked, pressing her body to mine and reaching down my pants. For an answer, I just groaned and she won the argument, as usual, by blowing me so thoroughly my knees buckled.

Once I'd moved into Jody's brownstone, she wouldn't let me watch depressing movies. I'd sneak one in now and then, though, because Jody had a full schedule—she'd been appointed assistant chief resident at Bellevue. My own job was going fine. I'd actually gotten promoted and even put in some overtime now and then, but I still found myself home alone a great many evenings. So one night I rented that movie Gary Oldman made, *Nil by Mouth,* which was not unlike a Mike Leigh movie, only harsher, and so very much like a lot of my life, yet somehow doing me good. It was a release to watch all this depicted on the screen, like seeing it there was getting it out of me. But Jody came home early and caught me and threw a fit. A total fit.

She said it just wasn't good for my mental well-being. She was really worked up about it and when I tried to reach my hand under her blouse, she swatted me away. I reminded her that I was a changed man. I was back with my old shrink, the psychoanalyst. Work was going fine. And our marriage was good, wasn't it? Wasn't she my best friend, my lover, my Jody?

She shook her head, though. She wasn't buying it. She said she couldn't trust me if every time she turned her back I went and rented one of those movies and stewed in my own juices.

"Look, why don't we get a dog?" I said then, out of the blue, because she'd backed me into a corner and I didn't know what to do with what she was hurling at me. And I knew she was frustrated over not being able to adopt Gabriel but I also knew she didn't want kids of her own, at least not then, so the next logical thing was a dog. And so I threw that at her.

She was stunned for a minute.

"What kind of dog?" she said then, melting quite suddenly, turning into the little girl.

"I don't know, you decide," I said.

"An Australian Cattle Dog?" she said then, her eyes getting soft.

"Sure, that sounds great, baby," I said, reaching for her, then letting out this big inner sigh of relief when she let me take hold of her.

"And we'll name him Craig?" she said, sitting in my lap now.

"Craig sounds good," I said.

"Okay," she said.

"Okay," I said back.

MONKEYS

By the time I get back to Fortieth Street, I'm dead tired. I climb the stairs, unlock the door, and release Katie's cat, Buddy, from the duffel bag I've got him in. Katie, my girlfriend, wouldn't be happy if she knew that I not only earn my living shoplifting and scamming tourists in Chinatown, but also use her cat as an aid in this, making Buddy perch on my shoulder when I'm trying to convince some couple from Holland that I can show them to an authentic Chinese opium den. Having Buddy with me seems to alleviate any suspicions my victims have and Buddy has really taken to the work now that my own cat put on so much weight she can't perch on me anymore.

I go into the kitchen to feed Buddy and the other cats, all of them clamoring loudly, making me feel like some demented cat guy as I put tuna into their bowls then stand there watching them devour the stuff. I give them fresh water then head into the living room to relax for a minute. Which is when I notice a man sitting on the couch.

Katie has a habit of inviting half the world over to our place but she usually doesn't leave anyone here unattended.

"Hello?" I say to the guy's back. He doesn't turn around, though. Maybe he's deaf. I come to stand in front of him and he looks up at me. "Hi there," he says.

He's a big guy with bright blue eyes. He's smoking a cigarette. Filterless. Mexican or something. Horrible smelling.

"You're a friend of Katie's?"

"Something like that," he says thoughtfully.

"Katie's home from work already? What, she went to the store?" I ask him.

"I have no idea."

"When did she leave?"

"Couldn't tell you that either." The guy shakes his head, then stubs his cigarette out in Katie's Holiday Inn ashtray. My girlfriend has a rigorous moral code but it does not prohibit the stealing of ashtrays—which she does obsessively. We have about forty ashtrays.

"I don't understand," I say, frowning at the guy. He has white hair, which makes me think he's close to sixty, but he's probably only in his late forties.

"Who are you?" he asks me, politely enough, but it's hardly a polite question.

"I'm Jack. Who did you think I was?"

"Jack?"

"Right. And you are?"

"Bob."

"Hello, Bob," I say, extending a hand, although the guy is definitely behaving strangely.

"So I don't get it," I say as we shake hands. "Katie just left you here and didn't tell you when she was coming back?"

"Not exactly, no," he says. "Are you Katie's boyfriend?" he asks me.

"I am."

"Live-in boyfriend?"

"Right. And you are?"

"Like I said, I'm Bob. Katie and I were seeing each other last year. But I had to leave town. "

"I see," I say.

"Katie didn't tell you where she was going?" I ask the guy now.

"Katie doesn't know I'm here."

"How's that?"

"I let myself in," he says, fishing a set of keys from his pocket and dangling them in front of me.

"Jesus. Well. You could have called."

"I just used to show up. She never minded."

"She didn't?" I'm appalled but I try not to show it, try not to let the guy see how badly all this is shaking me.

"You know Katie," he says. "Easy come, easy go." He shrugs.

I don't like the way he says *come*.

"I hope I haven't upset you. I didn't realize Katie was living with someone. I never would have come."

That word again.

"I'm not here to break up your happy home, Jack. Providing you have a happy home."

"Yeah, we have a very happy home," I say menacingly and I just stand there. My stomach starts to produce weird juices and I feel like I might throw up. But I can't let this guy see how bothered I am. I've got to act nonchalant. Like this happens every day. Katie and I just invite every single maniac we ever fucked to come over and loll on our couch.

"So. What can I do for you, Bob?"

"Not much, I guess, Jack. I take it you want me to leave."

"Well, Bob, I can't see as there's much purpose in your hanging around."

"Would you mind if I waited for Katie?"

"I would, Bob. I really would."

"Okay, all right, I get it. No need to get upset, Jack."

"Right, Bob. Nobody's upset."

"You're a nice guy, Jack," Bob decrees now. "I'm glad she's found someone like you. She's quite a girl."

"Sure," I say through clenched teeth.

Bob stands up. His head nearly hits the ceiling. I notice a scar on his neck. Looks like a Columbian Necktie. Like the guy did time. Or rubbed some drug dealers the wrong way.

I escort Bob to the door.

"Well," he says, pausing, "you'll give Katie my best."

"Oh, sure," I tell him.

Bob smiles. He has very big teeth. Very clean big teeth. Annoyingly clean. I hate him for his teeth.

"If you don't mind, I'd like those keys back," I tell him.

"Oh, right, of course," Bob says and slowly fishes the keys from his pocket. "Best of luck to you, Jack," he adds, showing teeth again as he hands me the keys and walks out.

I close the door behind him. I'm shaking. I'm overreacting. Bob's just a residual mess from Katie's past. It's not like she invited him over. The guy's obviously a sociopath. So what the hell was Katie doing with him? Does she have a thing for criminals? She doesn't even know I'm one. Or does she?

Next thing I know, I'm in our bedroom and I've thrown open the closet door. Packed in the very back of the closet are Katie's precious shoe boxes. Her personal things. Old love letters and such. Or so I've surmised. I found the boxes one day by accident when we were cleaning. She told me they were "personal items" and I left it at that.

I rip the shoe boxes out of the closet. I need to know what went on with Katie before I came along.

I open the first box. Sure enough. Letters and scraps of paper. I lift up a handful of letters and out falls a photo. Of none other than Bob.

He is standing on a yacht. He's dressed all in white. He's beaming a smile, exposing those infernal teeth of his.

I read the letter. It's very short.

K:

> *Just left Aruba. They're having a beautiful spring here this year. The sea is an odd green. Hope to see you soon.*
>
> *Yours,*
>
> *Robert*

My girlfriend has a whole past I know nothing about. Not just Bob. There are others. Other letters. Other photos. A scraggly-looking individual sitting naked in Katie's apartment; a black guy who looks about fifteen; some blonde bozo with long hair. I fan the letters and photos out all over the floor. My whole body is shaking. Why is she saving this shit. Like a collector. Like a fucking serial killer.

I pick the letters up. I put them in a stack. I want to burn them. I want to burn off the imprints of everyone who's been near Katie before me. I want to scour her.

Then I hear her key in the door and all my plans fall apart. I scoop the letters and photos back into the shoe box and shove it in the closet. I close the closet door and emerge from the bedroom in time to see Katie throw herself down on the living room couch, face first.

I stand watching her. I don't know what the hell she is doing lying facedown on the couch. I don't know if she's heard me come into the room.

She is so small. Her back is so narrow. I could just squeeze her hard and she'd break.

"Katie," I say finally.

"What?" She's still got her face buried in the couch cushions and her voice is muffled.

"What are you doing?" Something's off here. I'm waiting to rip into her but she's not herself.

"Winnie's dying," she says, lifting her face off the couch slightly.

"What do you mean?"

"I mean he's in the hospital dying. I have to go there. Will you come with me?" She's sitting up now and I can see her eyes are red and puffy.

Ridiculously, the first thought I have is, Isn't it convenient that her friend falls ill when I'm about to read her the riot act.

"Shit," I say, deflating, faltering, sitting down next to her on the couch. "Sure, I'll come."

She rests her head on my shoulder. I marvel at it. How she has no idea what's going on inside me. What I know now.

I contain myself. We get a cab down to Beth Israel Hospital. She leans her head on my shoulder the whole way down. I can't reconcile this gesture, this way she presents herself to me, with Bob, with her past. I know I'm blowing it out of proportion. I used to have pictures of ex-girlfriends but I got rid of them when I moved in with Katie. Yet that shouldn't mean she has to do the same. But it does. I want her with me on this one. I want us to be in unison, seeing eye to eye all the way.

We get to the hospital, find 17 South, and go into the room. There are four beds with the privacy curtains pulled around, like little cocoons of illness. I peer through the first curtain but it's an old skinny black guy with his eyes closed. We find Winnie in the second bed. There are tubes pumping multicolored liquids in and out of him and his head is small and pale against the pillows.

I barely know him. He's an old friend of Katie's. Found out he had the Virus five years back, then took sick three months ago and immediately became very ill. Opportunistic diseases attacked all parts of him. And I think the whole thing reminds Katie of her father, who died a couple of years before I met her. She's lost a lot of people for a woman of thirty-two.

There are two other women in the room—Katie's kid sister, Alfie, and another woman I've never seen before, who is sitting in lotus position on the floor. Alfie and the woman nod at us as we walk in. Katie pulls up a chair. I kneel at her side. I look at Winnie's face with its impossible translucency, like a Titian painting, and now Winnie's eyes flutter open and he smiles weakly and utters an "Oh," looking from me to Katie and then closing his eyes again.

Katie has reached over and grabbed one of Winnie's hands, and the lotus-position woman reaches for Winnie's right hand, taking care not to interfere with the IV needle implanted there like an enormous steel splinter.

A nurse comes into the room. A boxy woman who scolds us all for being there but doesn't threaten to kick us out, knowing, I guess, that Winnie needs us. She fusses with his various tubes and checks pulses and pressures. Winnie has his eyes closed and, I suppose to check on his alertness, the nurse tells him, "Say something, Mister Watson," at which Winnie's eyes open, radiant in their fever, and Winnie says, *"Kafka."*

Katie and Alfie and I start laughing like crazy but both the lotus woman and the nurse just look puzzled. The nurse makes a note on her chart and goes away.

Within an hour or so, four more people have found their way to Winnie's bedside, three sort of boho-looking guys and one woman, Winnie's sister, very incongruous in this environment, a very rural and Christian-seeming woman who is strained by the state she has found her brother in. Eventually the nurse makes a fuss over how many people are here at this hour. Katie and Alfie and I stand up to leave. Katie bends over Winnie. She squeezes his hand and whispers something. As she leans over him, her long hair brushes his face. His eyes flutter open for a second and he smiles faintly.

Out on the street, the three of us just stand there not looking at one another. Both Katie and her sister are the color of skimmed milk.

"Should we get a cab?" I say after a while. They both nod, still speechless.

I hail a cab and then we're zooming up First Avenue, and Katie is just staring out the window and I'm holding her hand that is so cold and small in my own and I want to scream at her, I want to fuck her, I want to do all sorts of things but I cannot.

The cab lets us out at Fortieth and Eighth and Alfie stays in and continues on up to her place.

When we come back into the apartment, Katie says she's going to take a long bath. I watch her walk into the bathroom and close the door. I stand there, at a loss. Like I've had some sort of overdose on emotion. I go in the bedroom, open the closet, and make sure I've put Katie's shoe boxes away properly. I sit down on the edge of the bed. One of the cats jumps up into my lap. I pet him. I've been diffused now, but I'm still angry. And all I can think is that I want to see my horse. I try reasoning with myself. I try formulating kind things to say to Katie, small consolations in the face of her friend's dying. But I can only think of how rattled I am over those shoe boxes. And I know I will let loose. She'll come in and put on that Elliott Smith record she listens to obsessively. She'll listen to the whole record several times. Lying on the floor, staring at the ceiling. Smoking. Failing to use one of the forty ashtrays she's accumulated. And it will be impossible for me to keep it in about Bob. I will rip into her.

Rather than go into the bathroom to face her, I leave a note saying I've gone to tend to an emergency with my horse. She'll be angry. Not as angry as me, though.

I catch the F train. It's crowded with kids, tribes of them, loud and gaudy and blind with lust, for one another, for things they'll never have. I take a seat by the window, where I can look out into the blackness of the tunnels, and I start to think about Ebolapox. Which is what I tend to do when things get bad. Think of some godawful something to help put my own dilemmas in perspective. Like no matter how fucked the thought of that Bob guy on top of my girlfriend may be, it should theoretically be small fry next to the potential decimation of the human race by Ebolapox. Say if some pissed-off scientist just loses it one day and unscrews the top of a jar full of the stuff. Releases it into the air, its tiny particles undetectable as they waft softly up through the branches of trees, borne by the wind into villages, towns, and cities, right into the lungs of humans, to roost quietly undetected for a few days before turning folks' flesh to Jell-O, literally melting their goddamned faces off as blood pours forth from every pore, as they cough up intestines and run around smearing themselves all over everything. Staining shit. What a fucking mess, right? I mean, that's gotta be worse than the thought of this weird white-haired FREAK on top of my girlfriend. Right? But it's not. I just feel like a monkey. One of those hapless rhesus monkeys they run experiments on, creating crack dens where the monkeys receive limitless supplies of rock and are then subdued with drugs with ominous names like SCH23390, and what monkey wouldn't go nuts getting pumped full of something like that, and I'm not some big animal rights Nazi going around dumping cans of paint on women in fur coats, nor am I obsessed over the ethical treatment of cockroaches, but it is hard not to feel for those monkeys, and right now it is hard not to feel like one of those monkeys, and I can imagine their little faces twisted up and their little monkey eyes slashed with incomprehension.

The train pulls into the Fort Hamilton Parkway stop and I emerge from the station. I walk up onto the footbridge above the highway and then down the other side to Windsor Stables, the ramshackle little barn where I keep my horse. I know next to nothing about horses but I adopted Rosa, who needed a home. I pull a few extra jobs a month to afford her upkeep. What's a few more ripped-off tourists or bartenders to keep an otherwise unwanted horse fed and alive?

I find the barn door locked. It's late now and everyone's gone for the day, but I know how to get in through the side door and I let myself in and flick on the overhead lights. Geronimo, the palomino that belongs to Desmond, one of the grooms, pokes his nose out over his stall door. I pat his neck as I walk by to Rosa's stall. I find my mare munching hay. She doesn't bother looking up when I come in. Horses are moody. Sometimes they like you, sometimes they just don't give a shit.

I stand looking at my horse and I'm so sick of every aspect of myself, including the fact that I work overtime to keep this horse but I've never actually gotten on her back. I just keep her clean and take her for walks, and occasionally Katie comes to ride her. And it strikes me as violently stupid. Almost as violently stupid as Katie's collecting mementos of all her exes.

I lead my mare into the aisle, clip a lead rope onto her halter, and tie her there. I go into the tack room and take the first saddle and bridle I see. I have no idea who these belong to, probably one of the several bizarre spinsters who keep horses here, any of whom would thoroughly flip out if they found me using their tack, but I just don't give a fuck and I put the saddle on Rosa's back, and as I tighten the girth, she tries to bite me but misses and it's a bit of a struggle getting her to take the bit, I've only put the bridle on her a couple of times, and she keeps yanking back her head, knowing that I'm inept at this.

Finally I've got all the gear on her and I lead her onto the street outside. It takes several tries to get my foot in the stirrup and heave myself up into the saddle as I've watched Katie do with such grace.

And then, for the first time, I'm on my horse's back.

It's a dark night. No moon. In the distance is the roar of traffic on Ocean Parkway.

I gather up the reins. Rosa pins her ears forward, attentive. I try to remember everything I've seen other people do. I think of Katie telling me how the horse senses every emotion you're having. Which would mean Rosa knows I'm pissed off and scared. The mare takes a few steps forward and it's the strangest sensation, this lurching motion, not unpleasant but a total loss of control. Rosa keeps walking forward and she's looking all around her, and then a critter of some sort, a rat or a cat, darts in front of my horse and she lunges to the side and throws me halfway out of the saddle. My right foot is out of the stirrup and Rosa lunges to the other side. I grab a fistful of mane and somehow manage to stay astride.

I straighten myself out and gather the reins and my heart is thumping out of control as I cluck my tongue the way I've heard Katie do, asking Rosa to walk on ahead down the street. But the mare spins around, trying to go back to the barn. I shorten the reins, pull her head in the other direction, cluck again, and squeeze her sides with my calves. Next thing I know, the mare is trotting and now I'm really fucked, getting jounced left and right and completely at my horse's mercy, and before I know what's what, Rosa has led us out onto the highway, toward the park, and she's trotting toward the traffic circle. Which thoroughly freaks me out. I pull on the reins, which in turn freaks Rosa out. She spins around so fast I completely lose my balance and next thing I know, I'm on the ground, flat on my back, unable to breathe. I'm not sure if I've broken my back or what and I can't hear or move. All I see is a peaceful deep blue. There's an ocean sound in my ears. I lie utterly still.

After what seems a long time, my breath comes in gasps and I start to make involuntary moaning sounds. And then Desmond, the groom who lives above the stable, is leaning over me, tilting his huge head.

"Jack, mon, what are you doing?" he says in his thick Jamaican accent.

I figure what I'm doing is fairly obvious so I don't bother to answer. I'm reassured to see that Desmond is holding on to Rosa's reins with one hand—and Rosa is standing there, looking at me, curious as to what I'm doing lying on my back in the middle of the street.

When at last I can stand up, I find I'm evidently all in one piece.

"You just had the wind knocked of you. Damn fool of you to get on your horse when no one is around, Jack," Desmond scolds me. For some time he's been egging me on to learn to ride my horse. I figured he'd be pleased.

"You got to get back on now, Jack, can't let the fright get into you."

"I had enough," I say, looking at my horse resentfully.

"Rosa didn't mean you harm. She was just dancing," Desmond says. "Up you go, come on."

I don't feel like arguing, nor do I feel like being a chickenshit, so I climb back on. Desmond holds on to the reins until I'm well settled in the saddle. He tells me I look tense. "Relax, mon, nothin' bad gonna happen now."

Easy for him to say. I steer Rosa around in circles and she's perfectly calm now. After a few minutes, I dismount and lead her back into the stable.

Desmond sits down on an overturned bucket and watches as I slowly take the saddle and bridle off the horse. I put the tack away and get out my grooming kit and go to town on Rosa, currying her with a vengeance.

"It's not her fault you fell off, Jack," Desmond advises after a while.

He's right. It's not the horse's fault. It's Katie's fault. So I tell Desmond what's what. Although I've never had more than a superficial conversation with the man, all of a sudden I'm spilling my guts at him. About Katie. About the white-haired thug freak Bob.

Desmond whistles through his teeth. "Not good, Jack," he tells me, "not good." He shakes his big head. He smokes four cigarettes in a row, although of course the stable owner, Gavin, strictly forbids smoking in the barn, but he's not around right now. Then, having made Desmond listen to my diatribe about Katie, I decide to start asking him about himself, about what he did before he came to care for the horses.

"Oh, you know," he says, shrugging and lighting yet another cigarette. "I had a family, wife and kids. I still have the kids but my wife doesn't like me to see them so much, sayin' I'm gonna put my bad ways into them."

"Bad ways?" I say, looking up from Rosa's hoof that I'm picking out.

"Bad ways all women think all men have."

"Oh, yeah," I say, "that."

"Yup," Desmond says, shaking his head.

I ask him how his back is holding out. He injured it a long time ago but just keeps aggravating the injury, what with all the lifting and shoveling of barn work.

"It's bad, Jack. Gets much worse I'll have to do a different kind of work."

"You can't do that," I say, for if there's one thing I know about Desmond, it's that he is suited to and loves his job.

"You know how life is," he says.

I shrug.

I feel a little better by the time Desmond heads up to his apartment adjoining the hayloft. By now Rosa is gleaming clean, so I lead her back into her stall. She goes in and does her little ritual, makes a full circle around her stall before burying her nose in a flake of hay in the corner.

I watch her for a few minutes and then put my grooming kit away, flick off the barn lights, and head back to the subway.

I get home and find Katie in bed, sound asleep with the lights on, and, yes, the Elliott Smith CD still going. I turn the music off. I look down at Katie's face on the pillow. Her small mouth is partially open and she's drooling a little. I reach over very gently and wipe the spittle from the corner of her mouth. I take off my clothes, turn off the lights, and get under the covers. I lie there, restless. I get an incredible urge to fuck Katie awake. It's one of her favorite things, to wake up and find me having my way with her. If I did it now, though, it wouldn't be so nice. A rage fuck. So I stare at her and jerk off. She sleeps.

The next morning, when the phone rings too early, Katie bolts out of bed. I look over to where she's standing, just nodding her head, holding the receiver to her ear. Tears start swelling her eyes. I jump up and wrap my arms around her as she gently puts the phone down and says, "Winnie's gone."

I don't know what to say, so I just hold her, rocking her a little like you would a torn child.

After a while she pulls away from me and starts getting dressed for work. I tell her she's nuts, she's much too upset to work. She ignores me, though, and ten minutes later she's out the door.

I plod around the apartment. The cats follow me, looking at

me, wanting me to amuse them. I take Katie's Elliott Smith CD out of the machine and put on Tartini's *Devil's Sonata*. I turn it up so loud I feel like I'm trapped inside a violin. I lie on the couch. I can't find the energy to head downtown and scam anybody. I just lie there. After Tartini, I put Satie on. Then Górecki. Then Joy Division. Then I want to kill myself. Or Katie. Or anyone.

Eventually, at 2 P.M., I go over to my forensics class at John Jay. My mind isn't on the lecture. In fact, the closer I come to actually getting a master's degree, the more I lose interest in the whole process.

By the time I get back from class, Katie is home. I find her in the kitchen, cooking fish for the cats, who are all gathered in there, sitting on their haunches, staring at Katie's back. She is lovely, even in her apron, even with grief distending her face. I hate her for this loveliness.

"Your friend Bob was in the apartment when I came home yesterday."

"Yes," she says, not looking at me.

"Yes? You know?"

Katie throws Buddy a small piece of fish, which he catches in midair.

"Next time use your own cat for your criminal activities."

"What?"

"You heard me, Jack."

I don't know how she knows. But there's no sense disputing it.

"What about Bob?" I say, feeling my use of Buddy for scamming is a pretty minor infraction compared to Bob.

"What *about* Bob?"

"What was he doing in our apartment?"

"He's a friend of mine, Jack."

"So I should just start giving out keys to my ex-girlfriends? Have them let themselves in whenever?"

"I'm sorry. He shouldn't have done that."

"No, he shouldn't have."

"I'm going to go to Cuba with him."

"You're WHAT?"

"He's invited me sailing. On his boat. We'll end up in Cuba. It's strictly platonic, Jack, please don't freak out. I know you're going to freak out, but you mustn't," she says, finally looking at me.

"You're going SAILING with that FREAK? What? When?"

"Tomorrow. I have to get my head together. It's not about you and me. It's just that I have to go somewhere and be calm."

"With that THUG you used to FUCK? Are you out of your mind?"

"Jack, you have to be reasonable."

"Says WHO? Katie, come ON, grow the FUCK up, people just don't do that, you just don't go SAILING with some guy you used to FUCK when you're living with ME."

"I have to. It doesn't mean anything about YOU. It's not about YOU. It's about ME. I haven't dealt with some things. I need to be at sea."

"What are you talking about, 'I need to be at sea'? When the fuck have you ever been at sea before?"

"With Bob," she says, shrugging. "He knows I'm not going to sleep with him. He enjoys my company."

"Katie, this is the most grotesque thing I've ever heard."

"I knew you wouldn't like it, but I didn't think you'd take it like this, Jack. We're adults. You should trust me. We have a life together. I love you. I just need to go away."

"You don't need to go away from someone you love."

"I do."

"Then something's wrong. Then it's over. It's Buddy isn't it? I didn't know you knew. But I'll stop. I won't do anything illegal with your cat. I won't do anything illegal, period. Although maybe that's what turns you on. Bob's some kind of drug dealer, isn't he?"

"Jack, no, please, listen to me."

"Fuck you. You want to run off with your lout friend, be my guest. But don't expect me to wait around."

"What are you talking about?"

"I'm out of here," I say, staring at her, trying to will her to melt into the floor. "If you think I'm gonna stay here tending to your goddamned menagerie while you go gallivanting with some sixty-year-old criminal, you're dead wrong."

"Jack!" she says, and bless her heart, she's actually shocked. She's fucking shocked that I object to her going SAILING with some LOUT she used to fuck. Women are nuts.

I can't take another fucking moment of it and I walk out of the kitchen, go into the bedroom, and throw some clothes in a bag. I go back into the kitchen, grab Kitten, and head for the door.

"JACK!" Katie screams in a way I've never heard her do. I ignore her. I slam the door behind me.

A few hours later, Desmond found me sitting in the corner of Rosa's stall. Kitten in my lap. Staring at my horse.

"Jack, mon, what are ya doin'?"

"Looking at my horse," I told him.

"Okay," he said, leaving me to it. About a half hour later he came to ask if I was ready to come out of my horse's stall yet. He was looking at me the same way I'd seen him look at a horse's sore leg, with pity and curiosity, trying to get to the bottom of the ailment.

"Your woman threw you out?"

"I left."

Desmond didn't say anything. Just shook his head. I didn't have to ask. He offered that I sleep up in his apartment.

"Don't have no guest room but I got a sleeping bag," he said.

"I've got my cat with me, though."

"Good, she can eat the mice," Desmond said.

The next morning, for a moment, I thought of going home. Of making up with Katie. But she was wrong. I was right.

I helped Desmond with the barn chores. The physical labor tired me out and kept my mind from doing backflips. Every hour or so, Katie would pop into my head and I wondered if she had really gone sailing with that cretin. Then I would groom a horse and stop thinking about it. The barn had a sort of freak-show atmosphere. About fifteen people kept their horses there, mostly women, mostly single and over forty. And weird as hell. I guess they were thrilled to find a new and reasonably attractive man working there. They'd all hit on Desmond already, but I was fresh meat. By that afternoon, three of them had asked me out. Even if they'd been raving beauties I don't think I could have done anything. I figured it'd be a decade before I went near a woman again.

After a few days, Desmond and I hit on an unspoken agreement. I did most of his barn chores, he gave me free lodging and some riding lessons. On the fourth afternoon after I'd left Katie's, Desmond and I took my horse out into a quiet part of the park. It was a deserted little field that wasn't part of the bridle path. Ostensibly we'd be fined for having the horse here, but Desmond had a way of sweet-talking the park police so he never worried about it.

Desmond was riding Rosa, had her trotting around in figure

eights for a while. Once he had her going smoothly, he dismounted and put me up on her.

"Hold the reins like you've got a bird in your hand," he told me as I gathered up the reins. "Like you want to keep the bird in your hand but you don't want to squash him."

I made a face at Desmond.

"Do it, Jack."

So I did. And Rosa dutifully plodded around, bored with the whole thing.

Just as Desmond came over to adjust my leg position, a woman materialized from I don't know where. She was a lovely woman, not much more than a girl, with extremely long shiny braids that traveled down her back.

"Would you mind giving me a hair from the horse's tail?" She asked me in a Caribbean accent much thicker than Desmond's.

"What?" I said.

"Ah," Desmond said. "You've got a wart?" he asked the girl.

"Yes." She beamed a smile at him and then offered up her hand that Desmond dutifully inspected.

"Jack, I'm gonna grab a hair from Rosa's tail," Desmond said.

"What?"

"The lady's got a wart. She's got to wrap a horse hair round it till it dies and comes off. That's how we do it in Jamaica."

"Ah," I said. I smiled at the girl. She was gorgeous, actually. I started to wonder if it would really be a decade before I went near a woman.

Of course Desmond beat me to it. He plucked three hairs from Rosa's tail and gave them to the girl, along with instructions on how to find his little apartment above the stable.

That night, the girl actually turned up and Desmond politely asked me to find different accommodations for the night.

I left Kitten with him and headed into Manhattan. I didn't know where the hell I'd go. I had my friend Willie, but I didn't even know if he was around and I didn't feel right about just descending on him. So I decided to go spread the misery around.

Her name was Angela and she reminded me of a weeping willow tree. She was a tall thin girl with long straw-colored hair. I don't know that she really did much for me on any level, but by then I had spent many hours nursing tonic water there at the Lakeside Lounge and no one had caught my interest. And I had evidently caught Angela's. She came over and carefully settled her long form onto the bar stool next to mine. Right away she launched into some story about how she had started out the night with her boyfriend of three weeks but he'd run into his previous girlfriend and just left Angela in the lurch and I started worrying she was about to get weepy on me and I began thinking I really shouldn't have bothered with this at all when another guy came over to chat Angela up, which is when I began to feel territorial about Angela and said, "Back off, friend," to the guy.

The guy was a lawyer type with a moon face and he was thinking of getting cute about it, getting defensive over this Angela that he'd said just two words to, so I took possession of Angela's hand and pulled her out onto the sidewalk and into a cab, which she didn't protest, and when I asked where she lived, her eyes swooned at me. "But aren't I coming home with you?" she cooed tragically, and I corrected her. "No, it's me that's going home with you."

Soon we were on East Seventy-seventh Street, where Angela was subletting the tidy two-bedroom of a guy whose wife just died. The guy had packed up and gone to Alaska to find himself.

The minute we were in the apartment, Angela got shy and just stood there nervously.

"Do you have anything to drink?" I asked, after a long awkward pause.

"Oh, yes, that I do," Angela said, making a coy gesture with her head, then showing me into the large kitchen.

The fridge contained many bottles of booze and one carton of orange juice. She poured me a glass of juice, only she was evidently not in the habit of watering her drinks down, for I took one sip of the juice and found it incredibly rancid. I spat it out all over the floor because if I'd kept it in my mouth one instant longer, I would have vomited. Angela said, "Oh, Jack," then bent down under the sink, I guess to rummage for cleaning products. Which is when I grabbed her ass. As her pink mini dress rode up her long skinny legs, I ground myself into her, then flipped her back around, and she said "Oh" again and I peeled the dress off her. Underneath she wore an elaborate lingerie item of pink lace that I just made mincemeat of. All the hapless crack monkey feelings that had been building were giving me strength, the way adrenaline in the face of fear would give strength. I just tore that pink lace off her.

Angela really looked quite pleased about the whole situation—in a sort of galvanized way—but then suddenly got coy on me again and slipped off into the bathroom and closed the door. I heard a rush of water, like she was pouring a bath, and I went to look at the rest of the apartment, a very lifeless place really, like there wasn't much life in it even before the guy's wife's died and he sublet it to this alcoholic willow tree of a girl.

In the living room were a great many books and I just started poking through them. There were different editions of Camus's books, some in French, others in translation, and I picked up a French *L'Étranger* and sat down on the floor and just stared at that first sentence that everyone always talks about. Katie talks about that sentence, and my former girlfriend Jody talked about that sentence, and before her, one or two of the girls who were one-night stands or three-week flings had also discussed this sentence: *"Aujourd'hui, maman est morte. Ou peut-être hier, je ne sais pas."* And it's two sentences, actually. But Katie always spoke of it like it was one, and I just went along with it, which is how much I believed in her, I just believed it was one sentence, and I know this is just the most absurd thing I could be thinking and surely now the girl Angela had drowned in that bathroom.

Finally I just walked into the bathroom. Angela was in the tub with water up to her tits. Her eyes were closed.

"Hey, hey there, you, Angela," I said, but she didn't respond. So I just got in the bathtub with her. Just like that, with all my clothes on and even my shoes, my cheap brown oxfords, I just got in the tub and it started overflowing a little as I moved toward Angela, as I reached for Angela's tidy little snatch there in the tepid bathwater, and I started jerking her off like that and her eyes were still closed even though I was working very diligently to waken her. After a long time she stirred slightly but was not truly responding. Finally I ended up standing back up in the tub. My clothes were soaked and I slowly pulled my heavy wet pants down, and with considerable effort—what with this tub not being a huge one—I leaned my body over Angela's and stuck my cock in her mouth. This succeeded in waking her more than my digital stimulation had. After a while, she was blowing me quite nicely and I politely pulled out of her mouth and shot off into the bathtub and then Angela just blithely went back to sleep, and really not feeling so good about life, I stepped out of the tub, leaving my wet pants in a pile on the floor.

I went into one of the bedrooms, where thankfully the guy whose apartment this was had left some clothes behind. The guy was evidently shorter than me, so the pants were pretty ridiculously short. I found a button-down white shirt that was just a bit tight and I put my jacket on over that and my wet shoes were still wet but so what, and with a lipstick that Angela had left on the kitchen table next to an empty vodka bottle, I wrote *"Bye bye"* on a paper napkin and I went, emerging onto Seventy-seventh Street and finding my way to the subway.

Later in the day, as I muck out stalls and wash out the horses' water buckets, I get to feeling shitty about the whole situation, not that Angela probably remembers or is wounded by a bit of it, just that it doesn't sit well in my little monkey brain. And it's no help to find Desmond waxing rhapsodic over Giselle, the horsetail-plucking beauty. All of it just serves to throw me lower than low. I realize I have to somehow pull myself up, either have a drink or an A.A. meeting, and surprising myself most of all, I opt for the latter. When I've finished up the barn chores I tell Desmond I'll be out fairly late and I head into Manhattan, to an A.A. meeting over on East Nineteenth Street, where I know I will be safe, where all the people are about eighty years old and have been sober half their lives and some of them even remember the founders of A.A. and are just loaded with wisdom and insights into their personal plights and those of the world at large.

A worn Irish guy is telling his story: Growing up in Dublin, his father owning a pub, and the guy drinking long before he'd ever had thoughts of women or of the world around him, and the only thing really that kept any sense in his life was this dog they had, this dog they trained to jump through hoops there in their yard at the north end of Dublin, and the day the guy endangered his dog, getting drunk and then asking his dog to jump over a stick he'd set on fire, and the dog's fur catching fire, the dog itself catching fire and getting severely burned and being thereafter a changed dog, that was the day the guy went off the deep end and lost any semblance of functioning like a normal human being, and it just got worse and worse until he got to living on the streets or in a flophouse whenever he could come up with the money required for bed space, and in yet another of those insane and uncanny twists that life throws at you sometimes, one day the guy was lying drunk in the street and came to to find a dog licking his face, a dog that reminded him of the childhood dog he had burned, and the guy sat up and started talking to the dog. The animal grew bored, though, and started to amble away. The guy stood up to try following the dog and, uncoordinated in his drunkenness, stumbled and fell, actually breaking his leg and ending up in the hospital—where he was detoxed, violently and against his will, and much to his surprise, whatever he heard in those sorry A.A. meetings in the detox worked on him and he's been sober ever since.

Something in this, in the oddness of this guy having a sort of animal epiphany, makes me yearn and feel bad for Buddy. Like, the cat trusted me and I used him. And I need to see the cat and it's been ten days since I left Katie's, and who knows, maybe she didn't go sailing with the freak, maybe she is there, on Fortieth Street, lying on the floor listening to Elliott Smith, dropping ashes everywhere. Maybe Buddy is watching her.

So I find a pay phone and dial the number. And the machine comes. Katie has replaced my outgoing message and now her voice tells me there is no one at home. It doesn't say she's away, but then it wouldn't.

When I hear the beep, I try punching in the remote code to retrieve any messages, but Katie has evidently changed this too.

I decide this all means she is in fact away. She did go sailing. And thus her cats must be with her sister, Alfie.

So I take the subway up to Alfie's place on Fiftieth and Ninth. I don't call first. I'm sure Alfie doesn't want to see me. The downstairs door is fortunately open and I don't have to jimmy the lock. I walk up to the third floor and knock on Alfie's door. After some time, I hear her shout "WHO?" from the other side of the door.

"It's Jack. Is Buddy there, Alfie? I need to see him."

There's a silence and then Alfie opens up and peers at me through the crack in the door.

"I'm sorry to drop in, but I needed to see Buddy. I figured Katie left him with you," I say.

Alfie, looking none too thrilled, opens the door wider.

"Come in, I guess," she says.

I walk in and am greeted by Alfie's two huge white poodles—these retired circus dogs—and the dogs dance around, excited, and then the cats appear and I kneel down and look into Buddy's eyes, like there's some sort of answer there in that cat's soul, and Alfie is looking at me with her head tilted, a gesture that is characteristic of both Alfie and Katie.

"What's up, Jack?" Alfie says now.

"I just needed to see Buddy."

"Why did you leave?"

"What?"

"Why did you leave Katie?" she says accusatorially.

"I didn't leave Katie, she went SAILING with some EX of hers," I say, indignant.

"But she's not doing anything with that guy, you know that."

"Oh, come on, girl," I say, angry at her for defending her older sister's wanton ways. "You don't really believe THAT, do you?"

"Of course I do. She's never even really liked Bob in the first place. I mean, not in that way. She only had sex with him like twice," Alfie says. This is unlike her. The girl doesn't usually talk much and she must have fairly strong emotions about the situation to be volunteering these sorts of intimate details of her sister's life.

"Well, what the fuck is she doing?"

"I don't know. She's crazy. But she's not doing anything wrong. Besides. She's coming back," Alfie says, looking at me intently, studying my reaction.

"When?"

"In two days."

"She is?"

"Yup."

"She got sick of the old man, huh?"

"Jack, don't be a pig. She just had to do her thing. Now she's done."

"I can't believe she saddled you with her menagerie," I say, gesturing at the cats lolling on Alfie's couch.

"Well, it's not like YOU volunteered to help."

"Oh, right, I should have just hung around watching her cats while she went off fucking some guy."

"Jack!"

"What?"

"Don't be a jerk. It's just your pride that's wounded."

I say nothing. Alfie turns her back to me and walks over to the stove, where she's got water boiling.

I sit down on the couch and Buddy curls up on my lap.

A few minutes pass.

"Well, look," I say to Alfie's back—she's still tending to her boiling water—"I'm gonna get going now."

Alfie turns around, "Oh, yeah?"

"Yeah."

"What do I tell Katie?"

"About what?"

"All right, be that way, Jack. See how far that gets you."

"I'm sorry I disturbed you."

"You didn't disturb me a fraction as much as you disturbed my sister," she says vehemently.

I don't look at her. I turn and walk out the door.

• • •

By the time I get back to Brooklyn, Desmond is already asleep, curled up in fetal position in the middle of his bed—which is an odd thing to see an extremely large and forbidding-looking black man do. In the morning I get up and tend to Desmond's chores as he sleeps in.

I'm robotic. I'm not thinking about anything. Not even my horse, who is particularly friendly today.

That afternoon, Desmond ambles into the barn and tells me he's found a temporary security job at the nearby Brooklyn Museum. Do I want to officially take over his barn job until his back heals? I can work off the cost of Rosa's board plus make a hundred fifty dollars a week. If I want, I can even continue sharing Desmond's living quarters for the time being.

I'm startled. That anyone would trust me with the care of the horses. With the care of anything.

"Gavin will never go for that," I say, shaking my head as I think of the boss, an odd little man who's never said more than two words to me.

"It was his idea," Desmond tells me.

"It was?"

"Folks like you around here, Jack, and not just them horny women. Gavin thinks you're good with the horses."

Now I'm truly floored. Me. Jack McCutchen. Reformed drunk, petty criminal, bad boyfriend. Responsible for the care of twenty-two large and basically helpless creatures. So I accept. Not that a hundred fifty dollars a week will get me far, but it's not like I've got any major expenses these days. My tuition at John Jay is free as I'm on some self-improvement-for-reformed-alcoholics scholarship. And I won't have to pay rent or even Rosa's board. I can amend my criminal ways. Become another sheep in the herd of humanity. There are worse things.

I throw myself into the work. Determined to show Desmond and Gavin and everyone they've done right to trust me with all this. By the end of day two, my back is killing me and I think I feel my scarred liver throbbing in protest. But I actually feel all right about it.

On Tuesday, my day off, I go into Manhattan. Next thing I know, I'm in Chinatown. Like, although I haven't consciously thought of it, I'm going to scam a few tourists. Just to stay in shape.

I linger on the corner of Doyers and Chatham Square. I watch fair-haired overfed nitwits amble by, gawking at all the things Chinese. I don't have Buddy with me, of course. But I could pull something off, no problem. My disarming little spiel is at the tip of my tongue as I pick out the marks from the crowd.

I must have stayed on that corner a good hour. Just looking and thinking. Next thing I knew, though, I was headed uptown, and then I was at the Met. Walking up the huge wide staircase to the European Painting wing. I was passing by the El Grecos before I really realized where I was. Then I was startled. I hadn't been here in a long time. Not since coming with an old girlfriend, who, like me, had gotten pretty sexually worked up over the potency of the Caravaggios. To the point where she'd dragged me down into one of the little ground-level side rooms and straddled me, right then and there, in front of the thirteenth-century icons. We'd broken up that very same day. So I guess I'd been harboring bad associations with the Caravaggios.

There weren't too many people at the museum. I threaded my way back into the galleries, veering right and then right again, and suddenly there they were, *The Musicians* and *The Lute Player,* making all the other paintings look insignificant, and then, on the right, the newest acquisition, *The Denial of St. Peter,* which I hadn't seen yet.

I stood a few feet away from the painting, taking it in, walking up to it gently, as if any sudden movement would make it shy away like a horse. It was beautiful. My heart started racing.

The first thing that struck me was the tilt of St. Peter's head, cocked slightly toward his shoulder, as if listening to a sad inner song, which, I suppose, is exactly what he was doing. There was a strange orange glow to his forehead and he had his hands folded in toward his heart, this startling, for it is a gesture I've seen Katie make and in fact there was a lot of Katie in this St. Peter, or maybe I was just seeing Katie everywhere I looked. After a while, I superimposed her face upon that of the woman standing to St. Peter's right, but it didn't quite fit. Caravaggio's women are always dark, where Katie is fair, and I could feel my heart pumping in my chest, pumping for the glory of this painting, pumping for Katie. I walked closer to the painting. I was standing with my face just a few inches from St. Peter's.

I looked around me then. It was just before closing time and a young chubby female security guard was the only other soul within spitting distance. I glanced over at her and she cast her eyes down.

Then I leaned over and kissed the painting.

I felt tears come into my eyes. And I just let them go, rolling down my cheeks, slow, warm, salty as they met my mouth.

Many minutes passed and then something snapped. I started to feel better than I had in weeks. Less like a crack monkey. Less like an imbecile. And I knew that somewhere, maybe in a suburb of Detroit, a high school science class was being taught the basics of genetic engineering and some of the students probably had, for a mere forty-two dollars, purchased genetic engineering kits to clone things at home. I knew that among these kids would likely be one lonely kid with a perverse sense of humor who would in fact be plotting out some variant of Ebolapox, cooking it up there in a high school in Detroit, and maybe

ONE OF US

It was nice of my wife to get institutionalized so close to home. Although Green Briar's proximity to our house in Rye, New York, didn't make it any less of a psych ward. Nor did Jody's being a psychiatrist herself hold a lot of pull on the flight deck. Particularly when she'd been caught trying to hang herself. They'd had to put a straitjacket on her. And now, as I sat in our house waiting for the doctor to call, I kept getting an image of a female version of Hannibal Lecter. Not that my wife remotely resembles Anthony Hopkins in *Silence of the Lambs,* just that the thought of her situation was so horrifying that I'd started thinking in movies, which was something I hadn't done since my own tenure in the nuthouse. Which is where I first met my wife. She was my shrink. Then she became my girlfriend, and eventually my wife. And now it was like I'd vampirized her sanity. I'd grown increasingly self-confident and at ease in the world. I had few, if any, symptoms of neurosis. I hadn't thought in movies in a long time. Until now: I kept flashing on the scene right before Dr. Lecter kills and eats a security guard. He's got Bach's *Goldberg Variations* playing on his jail cell record player, and as Glenn Gould whips up a melancholy frenzy on the piano, Lecter opens a copy of *Bon Appétit* magazine and makes a graceful balletic movement with his arm that is one of the most frightening things ever. Next to knowing your wife is lying restrained on a hospital bed.

After a few minutes of thinking like this, I go so far as to put on the *Goldberg Variations.* I sit down and close my eyes as Gould's finger lands lovingly on that first G, fluttering up to the A, the B, and then down. Just as the bass part pulls hard at my heart, the phone rings. I leap out of my chair.

"Hello," I shout into the phone, panicked at the idea that even for a few seconds I lost sight of Jody's plight and fell into the beauty of the music.

I listen carefully to the voice at the other end but it's only a telemarketer asking me to switch to MCI. I listen for quite some time. It's my penance for having let Jody out of my thoughts. I let the guy exhaust himself until, at last, the call waiting beeps and I politely tell the telemarketer I'll be right back.

"Hello?" I say, flicking down the little toggle switch.

"Mister Smith?"

"Yes?"

"Dr. Colby here."

"Hello, yes," I say anxiously.

"We're going to release Jody. She ought to be all right now, Toby," the doctor tells me. "We've gotten her over the hump."

It's nice to hear Dr. Colby use as common an expression as *over the hump,* for usually, knowing that I'm married to a shrink and understand such things, he speaks to me in psychiatric jargon. When we first met at the hospital the night of

Jody's breakdown, Dr. Colby had laid it on thick about Jody's *Major Depressive Disorder with Hypomanic Episodes,* code number 296.89 in the *Diagnostic and Statistical Manual of Mental Disorders.*

"I'll want to see her on an outpatient basis for a few weeks," Dr. Colby says now, "but you can come pick her up anytime."

"Thank you, Doctor, I'll be right there," I say, hanging up the phone.

No sooner have I hit the phone's *off* button than it rings again. I pick it up and appear to be on hold and I suppose it's that MCI clown hanging on there. I sit there for a moment, hoping he'll come back on the line. I want to badger him. I want to ask him deeply personal questions. I want to force him to hang up on me. A minute goes by and the telemarketer fails to come back on the line so finally I hang up.

I go downstairs and onto the back porch to give Craig, the dog, his dinner. Craig looks at me, tilting his head at me the way he does, asking where his mistress is, maybe even accusing me of hiding Jody from him. My wife and Craig, our Australian Cattle Dog, have their own thing going. Maybe the dog is just a substitute for the kid Jody so vociferously wants to adopt, I don't know, but the dog's never taken to me quite the way he has to Jody, and now I tell Craig that Jody's coming home. This seems to make some sort of sense. The dog seems to nod at me and then settles down to eat his dinner. I grab the car keys and head off to Green Briar.

I find Jody sitting in the hall by the nurses' station. She's incredibly pale and her red hair is cropped shorter than usual, making her face look very long. She sees me walking toward her and just stares, registering neither recognition nor emotion of any kind. She doesn't say a word as I sit down and wrap my arms around her.

"Hi, babe," I say, nuzzling at her neck. Her flesh is cold. Her eyes won't meet mine. After a moment I take her hands, get her to stand up, and steer her down the hall. The fluorescent lighting gives her pallor a blue tinge. I have my hand at her elbow and I gently nudge her to the left as we walk out the main door. It's a lovely night, the air has a crispness that Jody so loves, but she makes no comment, nor seems to even breathe at all. She gets in the car and folds her hands in her lap in an uncharacteristic gesture.

When we walk into the house, the dog goes crazy jumping up and down, trying to leap into her arms like he always does. But Jody just looks puzzled by all this. She pats Craig on the head.

Jody gives me one faint smile and a halfhearted kiss on the cheek when I put her to bed. She lies stiffly under the covers and closes her eyes at once. I stand looking at her, reflexively expecting her to suddenly come to life and pull me to her. I watch the sheet over her chest rise and fall with her breathing. I think of the movie *Betty Blue*. The guy and the girl are completely in love. They fuck like crazy. They love like crazy. And then the girl goes nuts. At first she's just a little strange. A little overdramatic. Then she goes off the deep end. And dies. I turn away and walk out of my wife's room. Ever since we moved up here, to her late parents' huge house, we've taken to sleeping in separate bedrooms. Until recently we still had sex constantly. But Jody wanted to sleep alone. Maybe it was the first symptom of her retreat. Of her pulling away. From me. From everything.

I go downstairs and put Bach on. Craig curls up at my feet. I sit listening to the first aria of the *Variations* over and over again.

Around 2 A.M., I go upstairs and sit in the chair at the foot of Jody's bed. I watch her sleep until my eyes close. When I wake up, I hear her in the bathroom. After a few minutes she emerges, stands looking at me, then gets back in bed and pulls the sheet all the way up over her head. I go to stand at the foot of the bed. I reach for her foot under the sheet and squeeze it. She doesn't move. I squeeze harder.

"Is there something you need, Toby?" Jody finally says, without pulling the sheet away from her face.

"Just you," I say softly.

"I'm not here right now," she says. "You'll be late for work. You'd better get going."

"The nurse will be here soon to make sure you have what you need," I say, still speaking to the sheet.

"Bye, Toby," Jody says.

I wonder what she'd do if I crawled under there with her. But I don't have the guts to find out.

I go downstairs and make coffee, then go into the huge living room and sit. There's a picture of the kid hanging over the mantel. Like he's actually our kid. I stare at the picture and hate it. It's what sent my wife over the edge. Trying to adopt that kid. Gabriel. The five-year-old son of a woman Jody had a lesbian relationship with before I met her. The woman had a stroke and died six months ago, and the kid, whose father had long been out of the picture, was put in foster care. Jody and I started trying to adopt the kid. Only I'd been institutionalized for a suicide attempt and we were hitting a lot of red tape. Which infuriated Jody. She had always been able to get everything she wanted. With men. With women. With her medical career. And now something was being denied her. I suggested we make our own kid but she wasn't interested. She thought, and I tended to agree, that there were enough kids in the world as it was. No need to make another. Besides, she knew this kid. She loved this kid. And that she couldn't have him sent her over the edge. She started forgetting things and flying into rages. She barely ate. We still had sex but it was heartless, almost vicious, sex. Finally, three weeks ago, having not slept in quite a while, she wrecked her car driving back from the clinic one night. The car was accordioned but Jody was all right. Just walked away and went into a bar. Proceeded to get completely drunk and started a fight with some woman, and by the end of the night was just this quivering mess on the bar's bathroom floor. The bartender managed to look inside Jody's purse, locate her I.D., and call me. When I turned up at the bar to get Jody, she went nuts. Started scratching my face and reaching for anything that wasn't nailed down and throwing it, at me, at anyone. And she ended up on the flight deck.

I walk over to the mantel and take the picture of the kid down. I put it in one of the kitchen drawers. I have to go to work. The nurse will be here shortly. There's no reason to dawdle. But I do. I go back into the living room and put on the *Goldberg Variations* again. I have plenty of other Bach CDs. In fact, I have several thousand CDs. I don't know why I have to keep listening to a piece of music I know by heart.

I sit down on the floor and conduct the music. I make sweeping gestures with my arms. I flutter the fingers of my right hand. About halfway through the CD, the doorbell rings. I let it ring twice before I begrudgingly get up, walk to the door, and let the nurse in. She's a stout blonde woman. I point her toward Jody's room. I don't want to go in there again.

I watch the nurse slowly walk upstairs. She has on a traditional nursing outfit. Knee-length white smock. Hideous thick-soled white shoes. For a moment I picture the nurse going down on my wife. This pleases me. It would probably please Jody too. I don't know. Maybe that's all it would take. Maybe if I pimped for Jody she would snap out of it. Maybe this is all just her way of saying she needs extramarital sex. Simone de Beauvoir used to bring her female students home to Jean-Paul Sartre, who later in life was not only extremely unattractive but incontinent as well. Simone would coax girls into her own bed just as a way of getting them in the house. Then Jean-Paul would pounce.

I put my jacket on. I go outside and get in the car and drive to the train station.

A week goes by. When I come home each night, I invariably find Jody in the same state. Lying in bed. Staring ahead. This particular night, I come home very tired and I just want things to be as before. I want to find Jody back from her own day of work. I want to find her waiting for me like she used to. Maybe already wearing one of her sex outfits. The maid outfit. The gardening outfit. The dominatrix outfit. Or just plain naked. Lying on the couch. I want to go kneel down in front of her. Rest my head on her knees and have her rub my hair. Gently. Or not. I want her to shove my head between her legs. Or kiss me tenderly. Depending on her mood. But I just find her as usual, up in her room, lying limp on the bed.

"Hi, babe," I say brightly.

"Hi," she says lifelessly.

She is lying on top of the sheet. Her nightgown is bunched up at her waist. Her muscle tone is getting slack from lack of activity. Not actually fat, but sort of rubbery. And dry too. She hasn't been bathing or lotioning much. And Jody has always been an excessive lotioner. Runs up unbelievable bills buying lotion for every conceivable occasion: hair lotion, face lotion, body lotion, foot lotion, hand lotion, lotion removal lotion, you name it, Jody buys it. So, to see her like this, desiccated, just isn't natural. She has one hand halfheartedly at her crotch, as if she'd thought to jerk off but lost interest. Which, even more than the lack of lotioning, is a telling sign.

I go into her bathroom and look in the massive armoire she has packed full of all her lotions, pills, shampoos, soaps, and whatnots. I find the industrial-sized container of body lotion. I go back in Jody's room. I sit on the chair next to her bed and hold the lotion out in front of her face, like, take a hint, honey. But she just keeps staring ahead.

Finally I shake the bottle of lotion in front of her face and say, "It rubs the lotion on its skin or else it gets the hose again," thinking maybe this humorous quoting of *Silence of the Lambs,* this touch of levity, will perhaps snap Jody out of it and she'll sit up and do something about herself.

It works like a charm. Jody JOLTS up, her eyes get huge, and her face turns the color of skimmed milk.

"What, what did you say to me, Toby, WHAT?"

She does not appear amused at all. She's looking at me wildly and her heart's pumping so fast it's making the vein on her forehead pop out and throb like a gorged flower stem.

"Calm down. I'm sorry, baby. Easy," I say, crawling into the bed with her and throwing my arms around her. But she's so opposed to feeling me near her she actually jumps up out of the bed.

"I'm just trying to bring some lightness into the situation, Jody," I say, still lying on the bed, looking up at her. "You're a goddamned lump ever since all this happened. I'm just trying to help."

"Well, don't," she says. "And where's Craig? CRAAAIG," she howls out.

I take this as a good sign. She has basically ignored the dog since coming home. Our Australian Cattle Dog dutifully comes bouncing into the room, wagging his stump of a tail.

"Craig," Jody says. "Jump up," she orders him.

Craig jumps into Jody's extended arms and I don't know where she's suddenly found the strength to cradle forty-five pounds of pure muscle and speckled bluish fur when she's been lying like a zombie all week not eating or bathing or speaking. But she's got the dog in her arms and she starts spinning around, laughing as Craig laps at her face. It's some sort of major celebration they've got going, and this is ridiculous but I feel jealous of the dog, like he's suddenly pulled her out of the torpor, where nothing I've tried has been effective.

Finally, Craig squirms and makes himself heavy in her pale arms and she sets him down, but she's still got a leftover smile on her lips.

"Baby," I say, going to wrap my arms around her. "You're finally out of bed," I say to her, but this was not a good idea. She stands still and frozen in my arms and then I just stop hugging her and we both stand looking at each other.

"I have to do something," Jody says at last when we've had a longer staring match than I think we've ever done.

"About?"

"Everything. I hate it here."

"How's that? 'Here' where? What do you mean? Me? Do you hate me?" I say, feeling like a stabbed dove.

"Why does everything have to be about you?" she says.

"It isn't about me," I say. "Nothing is. Nothing in your world is about me. That's the problem."

"You loved me because you thought I'd fix it all," she says, narrowing her eyes and putting one of her fists on her hip.

I stare at her. I can't think of what to say.

"It's true. You know it is," my wife says.

"It started that way," I concede, "but then it got to be more. Very quickly. A great deal more. And you don't love me, you just love me back. You just accept what I'm giving out and return it diluted."

"How can you say that?"

"Rings true, huh?"

"What does this have to do with this house?" she says, making a sweeping gesture of disgust.

"What are you talking about?"

"That's what I meant. What I meant was I hate this house. Not you, Toby. I've just been institutionalized and now I'm in a different jail entirely. I'm in the house where I was unhappiest. Where I grew up. Where all my ghosts live," she says, looking away.

It's more than I can take, I'm so furious and confused and in love.

"We don't have to live here. I thought you wanted to," I say finally.

"You weren't making any money. I wanted a dog and some space. It seemed like the right thing to do."

"I make money now and we have a dog and we can go anywhere."

"Can we, Toby, can we really? Is there really anything between us?"

"Jody," I say, and it's all I CAN say. Just those two syllables. I don't know what's gotten into her. I don't know her. I don't know her at all. She's a psychiatrist who picked up one of her patients. And married him. A few months after a suicide attempt. You'd have to be nuts to do that. I know that now. I know more about madness now. But I don't know my wife.

That morning, watching her get dressed, it occurred to me that her skin was lovelier than usual. She had long since gone back to lotioning with a vengeance, but it wasn't just the application of cream that was making her skin glow, and certainly it wasn't me, because, although since moving to Brooklyn we'd gone back to sharing a bedroom, she hadn't really been in it with me.

I'd feel her body there next to mine, occupying the space in the bed, but Jody herself really wasn't there, she was off in distant landscapes where I didn't figure at all. We rarely had sex and when we did it wasn't at all the way it used to be.

We had actually made progress toward adopting the kid. We'd gone on several interviews and were now endlessly being investigated and spied upon, and so it was particularly brazen of Jody to be having affairs as she was. Some nights she wouldn't come home at all, and the thing that bothered me most in this was that she took Craig with her on these all-night jags. It's one thing to cheat on your husband, to clamber around other guys' beds, to drink until the smell of alcohol pours forth from your skin with each beat of your heart, but to bring the dog along on these excursions, well, that was just too much. And it occurred to me that morning that it was this, it was this fucking around on me, that was making her skin glow the way it was, and that just stabbed at my heart more than anything could have, the notion that her cheating on me was making her radiant. The cheating itself I might have stomached. The radiance I could not.

And so, that night when I got done at work, I went over to my friend Fred's office knowing that Fred and his boss, Olivia, a handsome brunette with a wide, almost American Indian–looking face, would still be at work.

"Toby, what brings you here?" Fred said after his assistant had shown me into Fred's magnificent office with the view of Central Park West.

"Just thought I'd pop by in case you had time to get a beer."

"Huh," Fred said thoughtfully. "Well, I was just finishing up here but let me check with Olivia, see if she needs anything else done."

"Invite her too," I said.

"Oh, yeah?"

"Sure."

"All right, then," Fred said, something passing over his ruddy face, some budding idea of what I really had in mind here, some budding idea that fully bloomed by the time we were all several beers into our evening at the Lakeside Lounge, which was just down the block from Olivia's very posh co-op on Avenue B, where, pretty soon, the three of us ended up, none of us big drinkers and all three of us therefore rather drunk, and Olivia showed us around her very swank home with the impossibly tall ceilings and each enormous room painted a lovely and vivid shade, crimson and teal and bottle green and a yellow that somehow was heartbreaking, as was the situation beginning to be because now it finally occurred to me that Fred also wanted to sleep with Olivia and that there was a definite struggle going on here, and as Olivia amused us by playing scratchy records from our youth, records from Iggy Pop's lost years, bizarre ballads and strange stiff rock songs and Public Image Ltd.'s first and third records and the Treacherous Three and Schoolly D, and then switching the mood entirely by whipping out Philip Glass's *Glassworks,* and the music building in a swirling and nearly nauseating frenzy and Olivia now standing there in the middle of her huge living room, she's kicked off her high heels and is in stocking feet with the tight knee-length skirt loving her slight curves, and Fred is standing right near her, sipping a martini, for now we've moved on to these, and all three of us were once hopeless, lost, and fucked-up people who listened to punk and avant-garde classical music but now somehow we've stumbled into adult-hood and into the sorts of lives we never dreamed we'd have, much less want, and we are drinking martinis and reminiscing about the first time we all heard Philip Glass, and I am sitting on the enormous and beautiful crimson velvet couch when Fred brazenly leans into Olivia and kisses her on the mouth and Olivia is so taken off guard that she nearly falls backward and then lets out a nervous little laugh and Fred takes two steps toward her, as if I simply didn't exist at all, and he lightly takes her wrist and leans into her again and she says, "Fred, no. Fred, please don't," but Fred is oblivious and now puts his arms around her and she keeps saying, "No, Fred, you're going to be terribly embarrassed tomorrow," but he's not listening, and finally I stand up and come up behind Fred and tap him on the shoulder and he turns around and lets out this little laugh and says, "What, you trying to cut in here, Toby?" and I admit that, yes, maybe I am, which is when Olivia says, "Oh, man, I can't believe this."

I wedge Fred out of the way and I kiss Olivia and at first her mouth is just hard and she is saying "No" and it feels like bumblebees buzzing against my own lips as I press into her, and once I have wedged my tongue into her mouth, once my tongue has touched hers, at last she ceases struggling, and one moment more and she is actually responding and I let my hands trail down onto her very fine ass, and now Fred comes up behind her, and we are effectively sandwiching her, and Fred presses himself against Olivia's ass and certainly this is not at all what I had in mind, this is not the sort of territory I've ever sought to explore, maybe two women at once but not one woman and another man, and yet it's happening, it really does seem to be happening, for my hand is unbuttoning the little pearled buttons on Olivia's tailored blouse, and beneath this she wears a cream-colored camisole, and now Fred's hand meets mine in the race to Olivia's fine and tiny breasts, his hand gets the left one, I settle for the right one, and as I go to put my other hand on Olivia's ass, I find that Fred has already hiked the skirt up over her hips and has one of his hands there and also his erection, which I accidentally brush with my hand and Fred actually grabs my hand then and puts it firmly on his cock, which feels rather menacing through his suit pants.

I have felt a cock before, even sucked one, but this was many, many years ago with a stripper girlfriend who was living with a guy that she made me suck off one night, this causing her no end of ecstasy as she kneeled next to me, jerking herself off and occasionally getting her own mouth in there, next to mine, on part of the guy's cock, but that was a long long time ago, way before my marriage, and although my wife is probably as sexually deviant as they come, since pairing off she and I had, until recently, kept to ourselves, exploring each other in a very thorough fashion but not other people.

By now, though, Fred and I have Olivia down to her stockings, lovely flesh-colored stockings that are quite silky, and Fred, to my distress, has his pants down at his ankles and his rather enormous cock sticking out and pretty soon it's quite a mess with Fred bending Olivia forward and entering her from behind as I squeeze her nipples and reach down between her legs, feeling Fred's cock do its work there, and after a very short while Fred pulls out of Olivia and shoots off and Olivia and I crumble down to the floor, where we become a rutting heap, and my fantasies of Olivia always involved something a great deal more genteel than this and a lot of her appeal was in my knowing she'd had a strange time of it in her twenties, ran wild and did drugs and fucked indiscriminately, but now she's a solid and beautiful and poised art director just coming out of a long relationship with an environmental lawyer, and I'd envisioned this sort of dignified affair possibly culminating in a slight drama where I'd have to choose between my wife and Olivia and maybe it would have been a close call, although I would have chosen to stay with my wife, and now it just hasn't turned out that way at all, and with great embarrassment, now that all three of us have come, we are putting our clothes back on and Olivia retreats into the bathroom and Fred and I just look away from each other and then I say that I have to go and for Fred to tell Olivia goodbye, and I just get out of there and hail a cab back to Park Slope and walk into our lovely brownstone, and to my great surprise Craig greets me, and Jody is sitting on the couch furiously scribbling something.

"I didn't think I'd find you home," I say a little sheepishly, feeling fairly confident that my wife will smell sex on me.

"I got Gabriel."

"You did what?"

"They're going to let us adopt Gabriel."

"You're kidding."

"You know I wouldn't joke about Gabriel," my wife says, looking up from the forms she is filling out.

Craig is lying at her feet and he looks rather pleased too, as usual, seeming to perfectly understand everything my wife is thinking, and perhaps I just project this onto the dog as I am so baffled by not understanding my wife, but they do say Australian Cattle Dogs are really some of the smartest dogs going and certainly Craig is clever.

"No, I guess you wouldn't," I say. "That's really great, baby."

"That's all you can say, 'That's great, baby'?"

"How else can I express it?"

"Come here," she says, patting the spot next to her on the couch, and I sit next to her and she puts her arms around me and rests her head on my shoulder.

"Do you think we can have a truce now, Toby, for Gabriel, for all of us?"

"A truce?"

"Can we try to be friends again?" my wife says, opening her pale blue eyes wide.

For a moment I wonder if maybe she CAN smell sex on me

and it is this, this threat of losing parts of me to another, maybe it is this that is making her speak to me in this way.

"Of course," I say.

"No, not 'of course.' I've been bad," Jody says.

"Yes," I say. And I suppose she wants to be punished. Just as, over the last few months, she wanted me to ignore her behavior, now she wants it addressed. The tables really have turned.

So I spank her. Pretty hard. At first just bending her over my knee and spanking her through the fabric of her skirt. Then I hike the skirt up. She isn't wearing underwear. My hand makes red marks on her ass. She yelps as I get more passionate.

But my wife's not much of a submissive. Once her ass has turned good and red, she scrambles to her feet, hikes the skirt back down over her hips, takes my hand, and leads me into the bedroom, where she very methodically ties me up. She starts to blow me and then stops. This is one of her favorite tricks.

"You've been fucking someone else," she says, looking up from my crotch.

"So have you."

"Can we call a truce on that too?"

"You started it."

"And I'm stopping it."

"Well, don't stop THAT," I say, grabbing her hair and pulling her head back to me.

And then the kid came, a smallish brown-haired five-year-old with impossibly large eyes. He was very quiet the first few days, not talking to us but at least seeming to communicate with the dog, this giving us hope, his face itself giving us hope, and so many things had happened between Jody and me in our short time together and so very many things had happened to Jody long before we'd stumbled into each other's lives, but perhaps none of it mattered.

A week after Gabriel arrived, we were in his room one night, checking on his sleep.

"Look, " Jody said, staring down at Gabriel. "Look at all the possibilities in that little face. Who knows what we'll do to him or what the world will do to him? Maybe he'll be a saint, or maybe he'll be a freak."

"One of us, one of us," I said, trying to be funny.

"Are you thinking in movies again?" Jody said, catching my *Freaks* reference even though I was really doing it the way Lyle Lovett does it in *The Player* more than the way the freaks do it in *Freaks,* but all these little subtleties were lost on my wife because I couldn't even mention a movie without Jody thinking it signaled a relapse.

"Look, I like movies," I said. "It doesn't mean I'm going to kill myself. Calm down."

"I am calm."

"I know. You are. And I'm so grateful."

"Ha."

"Ha what?

"You sound like a sap."

"But I am a sap, Jody. I love you. I love Gabriel. I even love the damned dog. That's a lot. That's more than has ever been in me before. I might snap from it. But not like in the past. I'm not gonna go nuts. I'm not gonna kill myself. We're going to be okay," I said.

Jody looked at me for a long moment and something odd clouded through her eyes.

"I used to date this guy," she said then, "a long time ago. A dermatologist. He was an asshole. But he lived next door to a

massage parlor, this place called Paradise, and people were endlessly ringing his bell thinking it was the massage parlor's bell.
Finally he put a sign on a door that said, *Paradise Is Next Door.*
But it isn't. Paradise isn't next door. It's right here. Tell me it's
here, Toby."

And I couldn't tell her that. But I put my arms around her
and held her tightly.

ABOUT THE AUTHOR

Maggie Estep's first novel, *Diary of an Emotional Idiot,*
was published in 1997. She reads and lectures throughout
the United States, Canada, and Europe and has made
two spoken word CDs. Her work has appeared in
various anthologies and magazines, including *Spin,*
Harper's Bazaar, and *The Village Voice.*
She lives in New York City.

Printed in the United States
By Bookmasters